A Friend I Didn't Know

Harel R. Lawrence

For information about this title or to order other books, or electronic media, contact the publisher:

Harel R. Lawrence

hrlmessenger@gmail.com

Library of Congress Control Number: 2020905833

ISBN: 9781386819813 (eBook)
ISBN: 9798624573833 (paperback)
ISBN: 9781078793070 (hardcover)

Special thanks to the following contributors:

Bill Wegener, cover designer

Elijah O'Donnell, photographer

Kim Chanwoo and Darlene Sullins, illustrators

Melanie A. Martin, editor and author of *"How Great a Canyon"* (Copyright © 2019)
(melanieamartin.com)

DEDICATION

*T*his book is dedicated to every person, regardless of age, who has ever been bullied.

Bullying in its many forms is one of the tragedies of everyday life. Being intimidated and harassed is something no one should ever have to experience. Bullying is violence that has stolen lives in more ways than one. Bullying is not just being pushed around or taunted in person; it also includes social media and online harassment. Faceless attackers can be total strangers who have decided to make it their mission to tear down others.

Even peer pressure can be a culprit, driving young people to do things they don't want to do. Peer pressure can lead to alcohol abuse, drunk driving, and even death.

We must stop bullying. We must call it what it is — violence, hostility, and intimidation. We must not be bullies to end the rage of bullying; we must consider the lives of others. Let's embrace our differences and find similarities. Let's show compassion and kindness. To those who have been bullied, this book is for you.

If you or someone you know is in immediate danger because of thoughts of suicide, PLEASE CALL 911 or 1-800-SUICIDE.

CONTENTS

Acknowledgements vii

Chapter 1: New Beginnings 5

Chapter 2: Gathering at the Flagpole 13

Chapter 3: Transparent Scars 29

Chapter 4: The Anti-Bullying Project 35

Chapter 5: Campaign Against Bullying 47

Chapter 6: A Time for Bonding 59

Chapter 7: Homecoming Dance 63

Chapter 8: Surrender and Revival 71

Chapter 9: Visiting Johnny 81

Chapter 10: Daily Life at Camp Change 93

Chapter 11: Adjusting to Challenges at Camp 99

Chapter 12: Countdown to Camp Graduation 107

Chapter 13: The Welcome Home Party 115

Chapter14: Johnny's Return to School 123

Chapter 15: A Night to Remember 135

Chapter 16: An Accident in the Night 143

Chapter 17: Reflection and Recovery 150

Chapter 18: God's Gift — A New Friend 162

Chapter 19: Graduation and New Blessings 172

There's Hope for You Today! 186

Testimonials 188

About The Author 192

ACKNOWLEDGEMENTS

I wish to thank the following people who assisted in the research, beta reading, and writing of this book: Christopher Leonidas, Deborah Brooks Langford, and Lisa Marie McCall.

I gratefully acknowledge the editors: Van Langford; Stacia Lynn Reynolds; Kristi Yokley; Matthew Neff; and, senior editor and formatter, Melanie A. Martin.

In addition, special gratitude goes to Darlene Sullins for the illustration of Johnny (Chapter 2) and to Chanwoo Kim for the remaining illustrations. I wish to thank Bill Wegener for his dynamic cover design.

And, last but not least, I give all praise, glory, and honor to the Lord Jesus Christ, who always brings hope to seemingly horrible situations.

CHAPTER 1: NEW BEGINNINGS

*T*he first week of school that hot and humid August would be difficult for the Hanson family. Indeed, it was a challenging, emotional time. Last year, before school started, they lost their twelve-year-old daughter to suicide.

Stephanie was a sweet girl, the youngest of three children. She loved reading books, daydreaming, and drawing horses. She was kind-hearted and full of joy. All who knew Stephanie loved her laughter and her long, beautiful, shiny hair.

One beautiful day, only a year ago, Susan Hanson watched her sweet Stephanie riding a horse, her hair swinging in the wind behind her. Stephanie seemed happy and full of life. However, nothing could have been further from the truth. Hidden from her family was Stephanie's inner pain and her possible plan to take her own life.

Why did their joyous little girl spiral into the depths of depression, enough to kill herself? How would they ever recover from this devastating event?

The family was shocked, devastated, and even angry at the suddenness of her death. Brian Hanson couldn't fathom what would make his seemingly happy pre-teen take her own life, in her own bedroom, much less. What had they missed? What had been the root of her despair? How did everyone miss the telltale signs? How did her friends not have suspicions? How could her family have prevented such a tragedy?

Such horrendous devastation rocked the Hanson family to the core. Their pain drove them to desire change — change in their surroundings and, thus, a move to a new town. Perhaps a change would help them heal? To better under-stand? To reach out to others in distress?

The Hansons decided to move to a midwestern town in the suburbs. Maybe it would be the best solution for starting over without their precious daughter. It would be yet another life-changing event — to leave their home in Cartersville and purchase a new house in Millsville, about three hours away, uprooting everything they had ever known.

So, the journey began. The family prepared to move, packed up their things, and said goodbye to their lifelong friends and neighbors. It was time to launch out into the unknown, with hopes, perhaps, for a happier future without their loving Stephanie.

As they arrived in their new town, Brian noticed a sign posted at the Millsville United Methodist Church. The church was in need of a new youth minister. Brian decided to stop in and speak with the senior pastor.

Brian introduced himself to the Reverend Ralph Cunningham and explained that his family was just moving into town. He mentioned that they were searching for a new church home. He shared how he had been a youth pastor at his previous church. His desire was to minister to students, where he could lead and teach them God's ways as well as how to treat others. Brian also shared, a bit reluctantly, and briefly, about his family's recent loss.

Reverend Cunningham seemed to like Brian from the start and thanked him for sharing about the unexpected loss of Stephanie. He then explained to Brian that several people had applied for the role of youth pastor. He added that the pastoral staff would decide at their next meeting who they would hire.

Brian prayerfully completed an application. He then left it for the staff's review. He knew that if God wanted him in the position of youth pastor, he'd certainly get the job. After all, his passion was students and investing in their lives. He had a personal story that compelled him to want to serve youth.

Several days later, Brian received a call from the pastoral staff secretary. He'd landed the job as youth pastor. Certainly, God had plans to use Brian Hanson in a big way.

An average-sized man, Brian was tall — about six-foot two. He had brown hair with some grey hair along his temple. He was well-kempt overall and quite meticulous regarding his well-groomed mustache. He wore glasses and had bright blue eyes, which seemed to be smiling most of the time. Yet, occasionally people possibly saw sadness in Brian's eyes if something was weighing heavy on his mind.

Brian was not your typical Wednesday-night-youth-group minister. He was a gentle, kind, and ambitious — a man with a purpose as well as a desire, even at almost age forty, to help solve today's problems regarding adolescents. He was inspirational, motivational, and determined in his life work with youth.

His mission was to educate people on the hazards of bullying, especially regarding children and teens. He was determined to help other students from being bullied. His goal, too, was to save other families from the same devastating trauma that his family had experienced.

Brian wanted to inspire young people to practice respect and to treat each other in Christlike ways. He also realized that some of the problems today's kids faced were drinking, cyberbullying, and school violence.

To be effective, he needed to show his presence as a church leader as well as a concerned adult, both in the schools and in his new community. He truly wanted to interact on a personal level with all the students whom he could reach. He began praying, asking God to help him be a steady and strong influence in the lives of some specific teens — those needing his leadership skills the most.

Pastor Brian looked forward to the first Wednesday youth service. He was pumped. He knew that first impressions would mean a lot. He recognized the fact that he'd soon have to learn all the names attached to the numerous faces in the crowd. He was thrilled to learn that attendance the first evening was approximately one hundred and fifty.

Brian began the service by introducing himself, along with his children, to the youth group. Standing next to him were Gloria, his spunky and pretty seventeen-year-old daughter, as well as Patrick, his charming and handsome sixteen-year-old son. He was so proud of these two, especially in the way they were handling the loss of their younger sister.

Brian knew that God had planted them in a new city, a new school, a new church, and in a new circle of friends to make a difference for the Kingdom of God. Brian was eager to see how his teens would blossom in their new surroundings.

Then Brian shared with the teens how just last year the family had lost Stephanie, who was twelve when she ended her life. There was a brief pause as Brian shared how his family was still trying to adjust to the huge change in their family. Silence fell over the room as he related how sweet Stephanie had taken her own life for reasons of which they were unsure.

To lighten the atmosphere, Brian expressed to the youth that they could call him "Pastor Brian." He added that last names were too formal; besides he was okay with the title of Pastor Brian.

He continued to probe the crowd with direct questions in hopes of determining what the students wanted to do each Wednesday night. He fervently listened to their requests and concerns, as well as strived to hear from their hearts. Brian asked God to open both his natural ears and his spiritual ears, so that he could truly be a friend to the teens.

One of the new students, a young teen named Alysia Sanders, stood and asked if the students possibly could hold devotions around the flagpole before school every morning. Brian replied that she certainly had proposed a great idea. He would first need to get permission from the school. He then asked if anyone else had any other ideas for Wednesday night.

Another young lady raised her hand. Her name was Patricia Miller. She requested a Bible study time instead of socializing. She and others desired to go deeper in their walk with God.

Amazingly, all the students applauded with agreement. It seemed they all wanted a special time during their school week devoted to going deeper with God. Brian was thrilled to know that these students were hungry for God.

Brian ended the first successful session with the students by sharing how he was planning a bonfire party so everyone could get acquainted. It was scheduled three weeks away, just before school began. He closed the service in prayer and then reminded the students to invite their friends to the bonfire.

The following day, Brian called the school to get permission to hold a devotion around the flagpole each morning. The principal told Brian that she would check with the school board. She didn't think it would be a problem since other groups in the past had used the flagpole location for similar group meetings.

Pastor Brian began to plan. He was eager to determine ways that he may reach out to these youth. He recognized he had a tough road ahead of him, yet he was determined.

He began thinking about his own precious Stephanie. Many thoughts began racing through his mind. He dreamed of all the what-ifs. Just what could he have done differently? Did he spend enough quality time with his children? Did he communicate well? Was he a good enough father to raise his other children right? Why didn't he notice signs revealing that Stephanie was in trouble?

Brian got a grip on his thoughts. He knew, in addition to his role as a dad, he now needed to focus on getting ready for the bonfire party. It was time to get acquainted with all the students now in his charge.

He made all the arrangements and sent out group texts to the students, reminding them of the party's events. He was eager for them to share with their friends at school about the fun event. The week before school started, Brian began preparing in earnest.

All of the arrangements came together. The event proved to be a huge success. Many adults stepped in to help and chaperone. The crowd was big. At least one hundred teens showed up.

The students had a great time of fellowship, in addition to getting acquainted with each other. They enjoyed snacks around the campfire, singing silly songs, and taking priceless selfies. That night, Pastor Brian began to gain the respect and trust of the students.

Brian began eagerly thinking of the next event. What could he plan? What activities or events might help him connect with the students? How could he build communication channels?

He noticed his son, Patrick, was taking interest in Alysia Sanders. His daughter, Gloria, was popular with some of the boys. Brian soon realized that even his own children were just as interested in making connections with the students as he was. Maybe this could be a family affair? Maybe connecting with the students weekly would lead to making great differences in their lives?

Early the next week, Brian began working on his Wednesday night Bible study lesson. He finalized a good format for Wednesday evenings — announcements, opening prayer, Bible study, and prayer. Then, he planned to allow the students to hang out and socialize for about 30 minutes after Bible study. This time would also include playing games and visiting around the pool table. Overall, Brian was pleased with whatever activities the students wanted, in addition to the events he'd planned. After all, the primary goal was to develop strong and purposeful bonds with the students.

Brian knew God would use him in a big way during the upcoming school year. Brian committed himself to God, promising God that he'd spend time daily in prayer and Bible study so that he'd be his best for the students. And, he wanted to rely solely and totally on the Holy Spirit for direction, discernment, and wisdom.

Brian sensed a spirit of revival among the teens. He believed that a revival that would bring more commitment from the students to lean more on God. After all, a revival could even penetrate the community and reach beyond just the high school campus. The possibilities of what God could do with such a movement were limitless.

Brian was thrilled with anticipation to see what God would do. He wanted to be on the front end of the adventure. He knew that to lead as God intended him to lead, he first needed to be a servant leader.

He was determined to both serve and lead the students and the community. He challenged himself to do so, knowing that God would guide his every step. His spirit was joyful as he waited in great anticipation for what God was up to in Millsville, and, especially at the high school.

The students began to open up. They shared and requested prayer. Numerous concerns weighed heavily on them — problems at home, problems at school, issues with friends, and, of course, peer pressure. The concerns were certainly valid, but they were nothing that God couldn't handle.

Brian pondered weekly the prayer requests that the students had shared. He spoke to Susan that these first few Wednesday nights and the bonfire party were just what he was wanting to begin to connect with the youth.

A determined Brian began to ponder how he could capture the students' attention as well as keep them coming to the flagpole. He just knew that the flagpole would represent a good place for fellowship, socialization, and a sense of community.

That morning, over his coffee and toast, Brian surrendered his request to God. He knew God would make a way if the flagpole event were to be a reality. He petitioned God to begin to set the stage for a very successful, Christ-focused school year.

CHAPTER 2: GATHERING AT THE FLAGPOLE

Brian Hanson awoke early that sunny Monday morning. It was the first day of the new school year for his children. In addition, his wife, Susan, just two years younger than Brian, was beginning her job as a history teacher at the high school.

After taking a warm shower, Brian gazed into the mirror, only to realize the first signs of aging. Staring back at him were a few new gray hairs and some smile wrinkles around his eyes. The slight aging of his appearance reminded him that he was almost forty.

Brian then dressed in a fresh shirt and pressed slacks. He went down the hall toward his teens' rooms where they were still sleeping. As he approached his son's room, he heard the loud, ringing alarm of his son's phone. It was 6:30. He knew that waking Patrick would be a huge undertaking. He knocked on Patrick's door as he heard the rustling noise of his son trying to unravel himself from his bed covers.

"It's time to get up, son."

Patrick asked, "Dad, can I hit the snooze button for just five more minutes?"

Brian opened the door and leaned in. "You'd better get up. You don't want to be late for school."

Patrick rolled out of bed and staggered toward the bathroom to get ready. Brian was approaching Gloria's room when he heard the sound of running water coming from the bathroom. He knew his sweet daughter was getting ready. Gloria was a bright, cheerful, and spunky teenager. She felt lucky to have landed on the high school's cheerleading squad.

The Hansons were like any other typical, middle-class couple struggling to get their teens up for school each morning. But, this first day of school, however, the struggle wasn't overly challenging.

Brian casually walked downstairs. The aroma of apple wood-smoked bacon, sizzling on the stove, filled the kitchen. He asked Susan what she was preparing for breakfast, as he tenderly planted a kiss on her cheek.

"Pancakes, eggs, and bacon," Susan replied, smiling.

After he'd had a few sips of coffee and they had chatted briefly about the events of the day, Susan asked, "Brian, can you go upstairs to check on the kids?"

Brian turned and headed up the stairs. He heard Patrick pounding on the restroom door and yelling. "Dad, Gloria is taking too much time in the bathroom!"

"Patrick, stop banging on the door. Gloria, you need to hurry up in the bathroom and come downstairs for breakfast." Gloria replied that she was almost finished drying her hair.

"All right, Gloria. Would you hurry up so Patrick can get ready?"

Brian then headed back downstairs. By 7:15 a.m., his teens were slipping into their chairs at the table. Susan joined them. Brian asked God to bless their food and their day, and they ate breakfast together as a family.

He polled his kids to see if they were excited about the first day of school in their new town. Patrick was concerned about making friends; Gloria confided that she was a little nervous about her classes.

"Don't burden yourself about being nervous the first day, son," Brian exhorted. "You'll make new acquaintances and meet new classmates. The important thing to remember is to be yourself. It will take time to make new friends. Just ask God to help you be patient."

Brian looked at his concerned daughter. "Gloria, I'm sure you'll be okay in your subjects because you're a smart young lady. Don't worry about your studies. You will be all right. Give your worry to God. And, I'm proud of both of you for being honest."

The family knew that the unspoken words that morning regarded Stephanie. They knew that the new school year would be difficult on all of them; missing Stephanie was still paramount in their minds.

Even though they were in a new house in a new town, their home was missing her joyful smile. Brian knew he needed to be strong and courageous for his family. He knew that's what Stephanie would have wanted.

Brian reminded himself that the move to a new town was just what God had chosen him to do — to pursue his mission to reach out to troubled youth. And, the local high school may just be the answer he was searching for to make a difference in the community.

The stillness in the kitchen was suddenly interrupted when Brian's phone rang. It was the school principal. Mrs. Jackson was calling to inform Brian that he'd received permission to meet up with the students every morning around the flagpole.

After Brian shared the good news with his family, he realized he was a bit nervous as well as optimistic. He couldn't wait to announce this good news to the students Wednesday night.

Brian began working on his devotional. He planned for some students to play music on their guitars and share testimonies. Then, in the last half of the meeting, the groups would gather to pray. Brian knew that if he could get some popular students to attend, others would join.

Brian drove his teens to school. Susan left in her car; she had to get to her classroom before the first bell. Brian dropped off Gloria and Patrick at the big high school and asked God to reign over the school. He then headed to the church, knowing he had much to accomplish and pray about before the students gathered Wednesday night.

Wednesday rolled around and Brian eagerly announced to the students that they could start meeting at the flagpole the following Monday. He asked if anyone wanted to play music at the flagpole. Several volunteers raised their hands. He said he was counting on the teens to invite a crowd. He reminded them that they could use the flagpole meeting place as a way to share their faith in a non-threatening and safe way.

Brian distributed invitations and urged the students to hand out the invitations at school as well as use social media to invite their school friends to the flagpole gatherings, beginning the following Monday.

Pastor Hanson arrived at the flagpole early on Monday. As he prepared to share with the students who had gathered, he glanced over and saw a young man sitting alone. The student was on a bench near the front of the school. His head was down and he seemed sad.

The student was slender with brown hair. His eyeglasses contained thick lenses. He wore a t-shirt that was ripped in several places, stained jeans, and weathered tennis shoes. He seemed quite disinterested in the other students in the schoolyard.

Brian observed several other students chatting. They walked by without even speaking to or acknowledging the teen. Brian took note as to how the other students chose to ignore the student who sat alone.

After the students had sung a few songs, Brian began the morning's devotional.

"Good morning, students. My name is Pastor Brian Hanson, but you can call me Pastor Brian."

"I'm glad everyone can support each other around the flagpole! Thanks for joining us today. I wish to share a devotional regarding life's directions. First, I would like everyone to please join me in prayer." As the students stood around the flagpole, silence came over them as they joined Brian in prayer.

After his introduction and prayer, Brian continued with the message. "When you think of your life direction, what comes to mind? I believe the course God wants every person to follow is the way that leads to salvation and to Jesus. Yet, we sometimes stray away from wholehearted dedication to Christ. But, we must always focus our eyes on Jesus and keep trusting God. Think of a way in which we, as believers, can live our lives by allowing God to direct our paths."

"The only way to achieve the right direction is to continue moving forward while trusting Jesus to lead us. Whatever our own goals may be — whether it is reaching out to other students, graduation, college, a job, or even getting married and having a family — we must trust in God. No matter what direction or path you are pursuing at the moment, put your trust in God to lead you and direct you," Brian urged the students.

He continued, "Everyone should ask themselves where this road called 'life' will take you. If your answers to this question are 'to Jesus Christ,' 'to salvation' or 'to heaven,' you're on the right track. If your answers are 'I'm not sure' or 'to destruction,' you may need to change the direction your life is going. Only you can answer according to what's in your heart. The time to change is now before time passes you by and it's too late to change. God wants the best for you and He loves you very much."

"When we take our eyes off of Jesus and focus on something else, we may have tendencies to sink deeper into our sin until we turn our eyes back to Jesus. Christians may not see what God is planning for them. All we can do is trust Him and love one another as we follow the direction he intends for us.

"The way God expects us to take is the path to salvation. And, we must live out our salvation day by day. Let's remember this Bible verse from Second Corinthians, chapter 4, 'So we fix our eyes not on what is seen, but on what is unseen. For what is seen is temporary, but what is unseen is eternal.'

"Christians can't allow Satan to distract them and lead them away from their destiny, which is to reach out to one another. Christians have a choice — to take the broad path, which leads to destruction, or the narrow path, which leads to Jesus." Brian continued.

"Let's listen to this passage from Matthew, chapter 7. 'Enter through the narrow gate. For wide is the gate and broad is the road that leads to destruction, and many enter through it. But small is the gate and narrow the road that leads to life, and only a few find it.'

"The choice is yours, students," Brian said. "Only you can decide to follow Jesus and ask Him into your heart to help find your life's direction. This morning you can make the first step. Choose to walk God's path for yourself and turn your life around."

"In closing, find someone you don't recognize and invite that student to join us around the flagpole. Help this student to discover how God's love can change them and how the decision you make or have already made can change you. The power to change lives is your choice to make if you allow Jesus to work through you."

"Let's ask God to enable us to continue to follow the direction He has for us. Let's be the leaders in this school whom He wants us to be. Let's be positive influences on other students. That's all for today. The bell will ring soon. Come up here and see me if you want prayer." Brian closed out the first session by asking the students to invite their friends.

The next day, Brian noticed the same boy wearing earbuds and sitting on the bench. The boy began to scrutinize the students as they gathered around the pole. This time Brian walked away from the group, in hopes of finding out the teen's name and asking him to join them.

Alysia Sanders said, "Mr. Hanson, where are you going?" The pastor turned around and glanced back at Alysia. "I'm going to talk to this guy and invite him to come over and join us."

Pastor Hanson casually approached the teen when he witnessed some students teasing him because of his glasses and his clothing. The pastor got closer when the students scattered, leaving the boy with his head hung low as other students passed by laughing.

Alysia approached Brian and he explained, "I am constantly amazed at how cruel kids can be to their peers." Alysia shook her head in agreement and headed inside.

Brian walked to where the teen was seated and asked the young man his name. He responded in a soft, low tone, "My name is Johnny Goodwin."

The boy wiped the tears away. Brian asked if every-thing was alright. He could not help but notice the tears and wondered how many times Stephanie had cried when no one had noticed. Small things kept bringing her to the forefront of his mind that particular morning.

He snapped back to the present as Johnny said, "I'm fine." Brian knew the teen was indeed not fine. As Brian walked away, he remembered that he forgot to invite the teen to join the group.

Brian called out and asked Johnny if he'd like to pray with them. Johnny turned his head and responded, "I'm not interested." The pastor turned to leave and said, "I understand, but you are welcome to join us anytime."

Brian suddenly remembered his own daughter sitting on the school bench that dark and dreadful morning. It hadn't occurred to him at the time to ponder what she was thinking. Now he wished he'd taken more time to notice what really took place that day. Brian thought about how many times his precious daughter cried, and no one even took the time to comfort her. Small things kept popping in his head again. What was the weather like that day? What clothing was she wearing to school? Did something happen at breakfast? He just kept thinking about the events that took place that horrific day. He shook his head and tried not to think about the sad events.

The pain and suffering she had endured because of others must have been unbearable. Brian soon realized what Johnny was going through and the pain he was probably experiencing. The youth minister needed to help guide Johnny in the right direction and give him a reason to smile again.

The pastor couldn't bear seeing another child hurt by other students. Brian thought he would generate a challenge to help Johnny before something bad happened and it would be too late. Mr. Tom Blackford, the math teacher, and Mrs. Sue Rawlings, the science teacher, walked over and asked if everything was okay. Brian must have looked worried.

Brian had a blank look on his face when he told them everything was fine. He explained that he was thinking about the ways of life. The way some things affect people and how certain events could change. He could not tell them he was again reminded of Stephanie and how the hurt of missing her was almost unbearable.

Brian then rejoined the group for a final prayer, adding a prayer for Johnny. Afterwards, he asked the group why the students were teasing and laughing at Johnny. Patricia, who was sweet, yet outspoken, informed the pastor that none of the students liked Johnny because he was strange and different from the other students. The teenagers talked about Johnny because they noticed he seemed unkempt and wore the same ragged clothes every day.

Pastor Brian said, "Johnny's in need of a friend. I suggest each student take a minute to speak to Johnny and invite him to join in." The youth pastor also told the students how important it was to stand up for others, such as Johnny, and others who are victims of bullying. He reminded them to inform school officials and the principal if they believe a student needs help.

Brian arrived the next day to gather with the teens. Johnny was there on the bench as the day before, only this time he wasn't alone. George Dillings from the group was typically shy, so speaking to Johnny was a milestone for each of them. George rushed over and told the pastor and the other students in the group that Johnny didn't say anything to him. The boy seemed to be disinterested as he sat on the bench with his head lowered.

Brian encouraged George not to give up, but to continue to talk with Johnny and invite him to join in. The pastor also told

George how proud he was of him for taking the first step. George said he would continue to ask Johnny to worship with them around the flagpole. Brian also encouraged the other teens to invite Johnny to join them. George was determined to make sure that someone would care. The others agreed to help George and continue to encourage Johnny.

Pastor Brian and a small group of students gathered to sing songs and listen to a message of encouragement. After speaking, Brian became even more proud of his son, who wished to share his touching and heartfelt testimony.

"My name is Patrick Hanson," he began. "I'm on the sophomore soccer team as a left wing forward. I'm a sinner. I struggle with being truant from school and skipping classes. Also last year I was charged with possession of marijuana for being at a friend's party. The police showed up and arrested everyone in the house. I was released because I didn't smoke the pot, but I was with some friends who did. When my dad arrived at the police station, I saw the pain on his face and how disappointed he was in me. I was put on probation and did community service for six months."

"While sitting at the station, I realized I needed to change. I gave my heart over to the Lord that night at the station," Patrick continued. "When I got home, I turned my heart over to God and was baptized the next Sunday."

Brian was almost in tears as he listened to his son talk about what he'd been through. Patrick's testimony was refreshing, a promise of knowing that God was looking after him. Pastor Hanson and the group of students said a final prayer around the flagpole. They asked God again to look after Johnny and to continue guiding each of them.

Patrick came over, gave his father a hug, and thanked his dad for allowing him to share his testimony. Then he also thanked his father for loving him and his sister. As they broke their embrace, Gloria rushed over and poured herself into her father's arms.

Brian told them he loved them both and said sweetly, "You need to get to class."

After everyone had left, Brian felt an urging to take a road trip to Cartersville to visit Stephanie's gravesite. The youth minister left a voice message on his wife's cell phone, asking her to call him during her lunch break. Then he stopped by the florist to pick up yellow carnations to place on Stephanie's grave.

Brain also called his previous pastor, Jim Walters, to ask him if he could come by for a visit while he was in town. Brian was planning to gather some ideas about how to help Johnny.

Later that day, Pastor Hanson arrived in Cartersville and met up with Pastor Walters at a diner.

"How is your family, Pastor Walters? And everyone at church?"

"Fine, fine. And, how are you and your family doing?"

"Well, thanks. I'm a youth pastor, and the high school has allowed me to share devotions around the flagpole every morning. I'm really enjoying it and I believe God has great things in store for me. However, there's this one boy, Johnny, who seems to be an outcast. He just sits on a bench each morning, outside of the group. How might I encourage Johnny to take part with the other students?"

Pastor Walters said, "Try to connect with him and get better acquainted with him. Another suggestion could be to talk to the school and ask permission to share your story with the other students at a school-wide assembly." Walter added, "And, keep trying to encourage the students to be friends with him."

After Jim and Brian had eaten, Brian stopped by the cemetery to drop off the flowers. He wanted to reflect on the special times he shared with his daughter. He gently took Stephanie's picture out of his wallet and kissed it. He spoke softly to her gravesite.

"Remember when I took you out on your twelfth birthday for a date? First, I took you to your favorite restaurant and gave you a locket. Stephanie, your eyes and smile just sparkled and you hugged me tightly in front of everyone. I took you to a movie and bought you a beautiful dress with flowers and a white bow around the waist. It was the perfect dress for your birthday party.

"I just loved our father-daughter dance. We danced to your favorite song. And, your smile. Your smile was fabulous, sweetie. I'll never forget how you loved having all your friends at your party. I'll never forget it."

Brian placed her picture back into his wallet and dropped to his knees and cried. He was angry and upset as he reached up to God with both arms stretched to the sky. "Why did this happen? Why didn't I realize she was hurting? Why, God, why?"

He got up off the ground, lifted his head toward heaven, tears pouring down the side of his face. "Stephanie, you don't know how much I love and miss you." The tree leaves began to blow, and he sensed a cool breeze come over him. He then felt peaceful, as if covered by a blanket sent from Heaven.

On Brian's way home, Susan called. He explained, "Susan, I visited Pastor Walters and then went to Stephanie's grave. Would you like to visit my parents for the weekend to commemorate Stephanie's passing?"

Susan wasn't sure if she was ready. She took a long, deep breath and said, "Yes, of course I would." Brian then called his mother, Emily, to confirm a visit.

Saturday morning, Brian loaded the van and they left for his parents' house. The children were excited to visit their grandparents. As they arrived, Gloria and Patrick jumped out and rushed over to hug their grandma. While Emily and Susan prepared lunch, Brian and his father, Richard, watched the football game on television. The teens went outside to enjoy the backyard.

While sitting on the couch, Brian and his dad talked about the teen who was being bullied at the high school. The two also discussed Stephanie and why Brian may have missed some signs indicating that she was having struggles. Brian wondered what could have been different if he'd examined her behaviors a bit more closely.

Richard turned his head toward the window and asked Brian, "What do you detect out the window?"

Brian responded and said, "I can view my teens playing and laughing in the backyard."

Richard asked, "Do you love your kids?"

"Yes!" Brian replied with a hint of disbelief in his tone. "Where is my father going with this?" Pastor Hanson thought. "I love my children."

Taking Brian's right hand, he looked into his eyes. Richard's aging eyes were full of compassion and under-standing. "God, our Father, loves you just the same way."

The words hung between them for a long moment and Brian didn't know what to say. Richard then patted Brian's hand and said, "My son, give your problems to God. He will help you work through the issues you're dealing with." Richard smiled and perhaps he detected something outside the window. Brian remained unconvinced. "Let's take a walk. I'd like to show you something else to help you understand."

Brian and Richard walked down a path in the woods. The son listened intently to his father. The two men sat on a bench in an open, grassy area surrounded by trees. Richard turned and calmly explained what Brian didn't understand about the view from the window.

"Son, I know how much you love your children. The time you spend with them reflects on you as a father. Take hold of this Bible and show me where it says life is going to be easy. We can't focus on the past because we can't change what happened; yet, we can learn from our mistakes. The view from the window resembles the reflection of your life as a man."

Brian looked at his father. "Why didn't you tell me at the house instead of out in the woods?"

"My son, we are only here a short time and it is important to take the time we have and share God's love with our children. The Bible has the answers. I knew my message would be more meaningful if we talked with no interruptions."

Richard took Brian's hand. "Let's pray and ask God to reveal what you need to know as a father." After they'd prayed, the two headed back to the house. Brian hugged his dad. "Thank you, Dad," he said sincerely.

Sunday morning, they attended their previous church, Cartersville United Methodist Church, with Brian's parents. All of them went to their Sunday School classes, where they were eager to see friends whom they'd not seen since their move.

After Sunday School and before the worship service began, Pastor Walters asked, "Brian, I know this is a bit last minute; but, would you be willing to play something special on the piano for the congregation?"

Brian told Pastor Walters that he would love to. He offered up a quick prayer to God, asking Him which song would be best. Brian sat at the piano as the crowd grew quiet. Gently he began playing "What a Friend We Have in Jesus." He played all the stanzas and heard a few faint "amens" from the crowd.

The Hansons remained after the service for the monthly potluck luncheon. They had a great time of fellowship, visiting with other church members, many of whom were thrilled to see the Hansons.

Brian was feeling quite emotional about being back in the same church that Stephanie once attended. He had a strong longing in his heart.

"Mom and Dad, we want to go to the cemetery to place flowers on Stephanie's grave. We'll meet you back at your house," Brian said as he turned to walk to his car.

At the gravesite, Brian and his family placed flowers on the grave and hugged each other as they stood quietly. Susan talked with Stephanie, telling her how much they missed her. Gloria knelt gently and placed a rose on her sister's grave. She began sharing with her sister about how much she missed her. Patrick then laid a rose beside Gloria's. His words were kind and sweet, as he choked back tears, telling his baby sister how much he missed her.

Afterwards, they headed to Brian's parents' house. Brian loaded the van as they said their goodbyes. Later, at home, they retrieved their bags from the car and went inside. After the kids headed to their rooms, Brian was still in a reflective mood. He didn't really want to try to focus on anything. He knew this season of grieving would catch him off guard at times, just when he was not expecting it.

After dinner, the family met in the living room for Bible study and to discuss the upcoming week.

Brian asked Patrick and Gloria, "Is there any indication to you that I'm making a difference at the flagpole every morning?"

Patrick said, "Yes, and we're excited about it." The children reinforced their father's eagerness and wrapped him in hugs. Gloria added with enthusiasm in her eyes, "Dad, you are creating an impact and, if we're patient with Johnny, he'll change his life."

CHAPTER 3: TRANSPARENT SCARS

Pastor Brian wished to discuss the problems of school bullying with the principal, Barbara Jackson. He also wanted to obtain permission to address the student body at a special assembly. He knew the principal would be receptive to his request and purpose for such an assembly.

As Brian proceeded toward Mrs. Jackson's office, he noticed Johnny approaching his locker. Roger Smith, Carl Fritzgerald, and Fred Carlson were standing near Johnny's locker. The three teens were chuckling and verbally picking on Johnny as Johnny opened his locker.

A few students banged the locker doors as they walked by. Brian heard one of the football players say, "Hey, Johnny, did you get a date?" Samuel Dalton suddenly grabbed Johnny's books away from him, forcefully threw them on the ground, and took off quickly with the other football players.

Three girls a few lockers down were snickering and giggling. They turned and started laughing at the comments directed toward Johnny. Other students walked by, strolling and laughing with the crowd. No one bothered to ask Johnny if he needed help picking up his books.

Brian could see the smirk on Roger Smith's face as if Roger's comments were meant as a sarcastic joke. Brian wanted to approach the students, grab them, and shove them into the locker. He felt his anger well up inside. He started yelling at the kids to stop bothering Johnny.

Brian then inhaled slowly to calm his emotions and walked over to the boys. He kindly and firmly told the boys to stop the harassment and get to class. Then, Brian overheard Roger Smith say in a crude voice, "Who does this man think he is to tell me to get to class?"

With the next class period quickly approaching, mobs of students were scurrying down the hallway to get to their lockers before the bell. A few students lingered next to the drinking fountain; others were talking on their phones. Several others were coming in and out of the restrooms.

The sounds of metal locker doors slamming closed echoed through the hallways. Pastor Hanson saw Johnny in front of his locker. He gingerly approached the teen.

"Hello, Johnny. Do you remember me?"

Johnny turned and saw that it was Brian. Johnny shook his head yes and then walked away, never making eye contact with the youth pastor. Brian was saddened that Johnny avoided eye contact; yet, he knew in his heart that someday, in some special way, he'd get to know this teen. He knew God had a purpose in causing their paths to cross. He was determined to pray for Johnny every day.

Brian continued down the hallway where he spotted Patrick and his girlfriend, Alysia Sanders, talking next to their lockers. As they were reaching for their books, Patrick glanced up and saw his dad approaching.

Brian spoke quickly to his son. "I just saw Johnny and I witnessed him being bullied. It was a few of the football players." Then he asked Patrick to keep an eye on Johnny. He reminded his son to let Johnny know that if he needed anything, Pastor Brian could help.

Patrick agreed to keep an eye on Johnny. Alysia also agreed to help make sure Johnny was okay. Patrick said to his girlfriend and his dad, "Johnny has been bullied in the classrooms, restroom, cafeteria, and other places in school. It's always those same guys." Brian then asked his son if he knew the kids who had picked on Johnny.

Patrick assured his father that he knew the students. But, he reassured his dad that they could discuss the situation more after school. The bell rang for the next class to start and the teens hurried to class.

Brian knocked on the principal's outer office door and asked the school secretary if he could speak with the principal. The secretary buzzed the principal's office. Brian heard his invitation to come in and he went into her office. He quietly closed the door behind him.

"Hello, Pastor Hanson. Please have a seat," said Principal Jackson. "What can I help you with today?"

Brian had his mental notes ready to proceed.

"Do I have your permission to speak to the students about the problem of bullies and bullying?"

Principal Jackson did not hesitate. She replied, "Yes, that would be perfect."

"Do you know about the situation with a rather shy student named Johnny?" Brian was curious to know the reasons why this particular student seemed to be a target of bullying.

Principal Jackson told Brian that Johnny was a fairly good student and was very quiet. The teen had some problems with missing class once in a while and she said that Johnny seemed to be troubled, as if something bothered him, but he never really talked about it. She'd suggested in the past that Johnny speak with a school counselor, but he'd refused.

Principal Jackson continued, "Maybe you could try to reach out to Johnny?"

Brian said he'd tried; but, thus far, had no response from Johnny. The principal then suggested that Brian speak with the school counselor, Mr. Jim Fannigan. Maybe Brian and Jim could find a solution together.

Brian walked intently to Mr. Fannigan's office and knocked on his door. Mr. Fannigan opened the door and said, "Come on in and have a seat."

Brian asked, "May I speak with you for a few minutes?"

"Yes, I have a few minutes to spare."

"How can I help you, Pastor?"

Brian introduced himself as the youth minister at the Millsville United Methodist Church. He then asked Mr. Fannigan if he were aware of the constant teasing and bullying that Johnny was enduring at school.

Mr. Fannigan said, "I've had no idea that anything like this has been going on, Pastor." Jim continued, "No one has been in my office about Johnny except for issues regarding his attendance and grades." Brian was curious about the fact that no one had reported anything to the counselor's office.

"Mr. Fannigan, do you have any ideas on how the school can prevent the students from being bullied?"

"I'm not aware of any resources at the moment. But, let's see what we can find." Mr. Fannigan then turned to his computer screen. He began researching some campaigns that other school districts had implemented — campaigns geared toward teaching students how to prevent and report bullying. To his amazement, several web sites and articles were quite pertinent to his discussion with the pastor.

Brian and Mr. Fannigan spent several minutes perusing the information they saw online. Jim suggested that they could gather enough information and try to put something together.

Brian added, "I think that's an excellent idea! I'm planning to speak to the students at a special assembly soon." Jim was pleased to see a parent be willing to plan such an event. He agreed to contribute to the assembly.

"I need to get busy with my day, but I will let you know when I have something. Maybe between the two of us, we can come up with ideas to present to the board."

Brian said, "I believe my own children are wanting to help with the campaign. I'm sure they would appreciate the information." Jim was very proud of Brian's kids wanting to get involved in such a great event for their peers. He agreed that the assembly was an important project.

After several minutes discussing Johnny and the topic of bullying, Brian thanked the counselor for his time.

"You're welcome. Maybe we can also get the teachers and staff involved. But, even before we get this assembly on the calendar, I'll ask the teachers to stand outside their classroom doors before school, after school, and between periods to watch the students. Maybe we can try to avoid the harassment you witnessed this morning."

Brian shook his head in agreement and said he'd make time to meet. As he left the counselor's office, he noticed it was close to 11 a.m. He knew the students would line up for lunch soon. He decided to hang around and join Susan for lunch in the teachers' corner.

Brian looked around the large cafeteria. He was quite surprised to see how many students sat by themselves or gathered in small groups. Several football players sat with the cheerleaders. He noticed a group of popular and outgoing girls who sat together. He realized that the students seemed to be divided into different types of social groups. Brian was amazed at how quiet the cafeteria was.

During lunch with Susan, and in a lull in their conversation, Brian noticed Johnny sitting by himself. A few other teens were throwing their lunch at Johnny. Johnny just sat there, with his head down, trying to ignore the teens, and eating his lunch as if nothing bothered him.

A loud, vibrant noise rang out across the cafeteria as Brian slammed his fist on the table and stood. Susan looked up at her husband. She calmly asked him to take a deep breath. "Please relax, Brian. Be calm. The students are staring."

Brian gained his composure, apologized to his wife, and sat down. He was perturbed, but, he knew he needed to handle his anger more calmly. The students began talking again as they ate. Brian was still determined to make his presence and seniority known. He got up and purposely walked over to the guys who were throwing food.

With a firm and direct voice, he told them to stop. He was polite, yet he meant business. He asked again firmly, "Please stop throwing your food at Johnny. Finish up, guys. Take your trays to the tray return. Head to class!"

The teens gazed at the pastor and shook their heads in cockiness. Then, they looked at him and didn't reply. Brian was still not satisfied by their silence, but, returned to join Susan. From the teachers' corner, he could still hear the teens laughing and making fun of Johnny. He turned to glance again at the boys and shook his head in disbelief.

Brian looked at Susan and apologized again. She had disappointment in her eyes; yet, calmly forgave him for his outburst. Brian, trying to change the subject, asked Susan how her day was going. She replied she'd have a huge stack of homework papers to grade that evening. Brian leaned over, gave Susan a peck on the cheek, and turned quickly to leave.

CHAPTER 4: THE ANTI-BULLYING PROJECT

Brian's first agenda item at home that afternoon was to get to his study. He needed to make the best use of his time; after all, he had to craft a speech for the school assembly where he would be speaking in front of all the junior and high school students.

Pastor Brian wanted to emphasize to the students the negative consequences of bullying and how the trauma of bullying affects everyone. Even if just one student in a school is the target of bullying, other students too are indirectly affected.

Brian wanted to get the students to help anyone they knew of who may be getting bullied, teased, or harassed. He wanted to stress to the teens also that it was okay to stand up to students who hurt others through harsh words and actions.

Brian gently walked into the living room. "Will everyone come in here and sit together on the couch? I have something to discuss with you. I'm scheduled to do a school assembly next Friday. Just wondering if you guys want to talk to your peers about bullying."

Patrick provided more information to his dad about the students who had picked on Johnny.

Patrick said, "I don't know how many times I have tried to stop the kids from upsetting Johnny. On several occasions, I witnessed some guys bullying Johnny, even in the restroom."

Brian thanked his son for informing him of who the students were. He leaned over and gave his son a hug, sharing with Patrick how he was very proud of him for stepping up to help another classmate in need.

Brian also asked his wife that evening for approval to speak about their sweet Stephanie. Susan agreed that it would be okay and hoped it would help other students understand that bullying can result in horrible things.

She knew Brian's words about Stephanie would be emotional for her; but, she also knew that God could use her family's sadness to reach others. Susan and the kids also agreed to sit on the stage with Brian as he addressed the students. They wanted to support their husband and dad and show the students that they too agreed with zero tolerance in regard to bullying.

Patrick and Gloria also wanted to discuss starting a campaign against bullies and school violence. The two eager teens began making posters and working on the campaign in hopes that they could help anyone who may be going through similar scenarios.

Brian watched his teens work on their posters with enthusiasm. He realized he'd never seen his two kids so excited to do anything together.

The doorbell rang. The Fannigans came to help with the campaign and share some of the counselor's new-found information from his Internet research.

While Mrs. Fannigan was in the kitchen with Susan, Brian called his children to come downstairs and bring the posters they were working on. Brian, Mr. Fannigan, and the teens gathered in the living room to share their ideas regarding the anti-bullying campaign project.

After a productive evening, Mr. Fannigan said that it was getting late and they needed to leave. Brian saw them to the door as they said their goodbyes.

Brian soon realized that his first assembly speech would be one of the most difficult speeches he'd ever prepared and presented. Giving a speech like this to students made it even harder. Susan could see the look on her husband's face and knew what that look meant. She had seen it many times before. She put her hand on his shoulder and said, "You will do fine, don't worry. We are behind you, Brian."

The next morning, the kids were ready for school. After breakfast, Patrick and Gloria showed their father the posters they had worked on the night before.

Brian was amazed at the time and effort the kids had put on these posters. And, he added teasingly, that he wished they would put as much effort into doing their homework.

Gloria spoke up. "Dad, we worked on these posters until 1 a.m.!" Patrick nodded agreement with his sister. Gloria and Patrick asked their father if they could also speak at the assembly.

"Yes, I think that is a great idea." Brian looked over at their mom and she nodded her head in agreement.

He then casually walked over to the door to kiss and hug his children goodbye as they left for school. Then he stepped into his office and sat down at his computer. It was time to work on his sermon. Brian was concerned about them and how to get his point across, but, he knew God would help him put it all together.

Brian composed his thoughts on paper as he did some research online to find pertinent information about bullying. He was quite disturbed over the incident at school and was having a difficult time gathering his thoughts. He remembered what his father, Richard, had suggested and decided to go for a walk to concentrate.

Brian wanted to ponder the encouraging words his father had explained to him. While he was walking outside, a cool breeze was blowing and caught his attention. He paused and looked up to the clouds.

He listened intently to the birds chirping as he watched squirrels running up the trees. He looked purposely at the cloud formations in the sky. He then concentrated on the traffic noise coming from the streets. And, Brian could also hear faint conversations of people on their phones.

Brian wondered how he could gather his thoughts with all these distractions, so he decided to head back to the house. He hoped to find a nice, quiet place to gather his thoughts. He knew this message was important and he needed to get it done.

Brian returned to his office, flipped on his computer, jotted some notes, and began typing his message. His trashcan was full of disappointment, as he tossed yet another paper into the overfilled receptacle. He wondered why he was struggling to come up with his message. He inhaled slowly and realized he needed a break. He wanted to speak with his senior pastor.

At the church, Brian hoped to get in to see his pastor. Brian knocked on the pastor's office door and asked if the pastor had a few minutes to visit.

"I do," said Ralph Cunningham. "Come on in, Brian!. Have a seat in this chair," he said, as he pointed to a chair across from a large, stately desk.

Brian explained to his pastor why he was there. He needed input regarding a speech for the students at the assembly. He was not shy about asking his pastor for suggestions.

"Let's go into the worship center. We need to pray," said Pastor Cunningham.

After they prayed in the stillness of the large sanctuary, Pastor Cunningham told Brian to first and foremost trust God. And, then he added that Brian needed to have faith in his own ability as a gifted youth pastor and to allow the Holy Spirit to guide his thoughts. In due time, the answer would be revealed to him, Pastor Cunningham added.

Brian was grateful for the encouragement and headed home. There, in his office, he began to pray and asked the Holy Spirit to guide his thoughts. He turned on his favorite radio station and listened intently to some songs.

He listened closely to one particular song. It gave him encouragement and motivation to begin writing. It almost felt like the Holy Spirit was guiding his direction, and before he realized it, he had his message typed out.

Time seemed to fly by, and before he realized, it was almost time for kids to be home from school. He walked into the kitchen to make a fresh pot of coffee and poured himself a cup. He returned to his office to read over his message. Now was the time to put on the final touches and make any necessary corrections.

The front door opened. The teens were discussing their experiences at school. Brian then heard a knock on his office door. Patrick asked if he could come in and share his day with his dad. Brian agreed. He asked Patrick to share what had happened.

Patrick began telling his father about the incident in the gym locker room and what the other guys had done to Johnny. The expression on Brian's face showed that he was worried and afraid of what he was about to learn. He sat glued to his office chair and continued listening as Patrick described the events in detail.

Patrick explained how the other boys took Johnny's clothes, threw them in the shower with the water running, laughed hysterically, and then started flipping Johnny with bath towels. Then, Coach Timothy Sanders walked in and asked Johnny what had happened. Johnny looked down ashamedly. He didn't respond to Coach Sanders, so the coach asked Johnny to call his parents and request some dry clothes.

Brian asked Patrick if he did anything to try to stop the events in the locker room. Patrick shared that he was afraid that the guys would do the same thing to him if he'd spoken up or tried to intervene in any way.

Patrick added later that some students shoved Johnny into a locker, and they were tossing his notebook back and forth to each other. He told his father that one of the other students told him about the incident and everyone else had just stood there watching from a distance laughing.

Patrick also shared with his dad that some students were discussing some ideas they had about the assembly. They were concerned if they should continue with devotionals each morning around the flagpole. Brian asked Patrick his thoughts on the idea and Patrick believed they should continue to meet. Brian asked if that was all. Patrick nodded affirmatively and left the room.

Brian overheard Gloria talking to Patrick about something and Gloria was yelling back at Patrick. Brian asked Gloria to come into the office and close the door.

Gloria came in with her head down. She looked up with tears in her eyes worried that she was in trouble. Brian walked over and hugged her then told her she was not in trouble; rather, he wanted to ask her about her conversation just now with her brother.

Gloria began talking to her father about school. Then she began saying that some of the girls were thinking of writing a note to put on Johnny's locker pretending to be a secret admirer. They wanted to set him up to be humiliated. She didn't know who these girls were because one of her friends told her about it. Brian asked her if she knew when and where it was to take place. Gloria replied that she didn't.

Brian asked if the girls had already given the note to Johnny. She thought they might have done so because she noticed Johnny reading a note, but by the time she started to walk over to him, he was gone. Gloria said she saw some girls watching him from a distance as they giggled and talked. Brian asked her if there was anything else she wanted to tell him.

"No. I think that's all I want to tell you, Dad."

Brian said okay and returned to his office. He picked up his coffee cup, but, the aroma of coffee no longer seemed appealing to him. His mind was racing with thoughts about the issues at the high school. He then waited in the living room, just pondering his thoughts, for Susan to come in. She arrived soon. He kissed her and asked how her day was. She told him she had to send a few students to the principal's office for throwing paper in class.

Susan asked Brian how his day was. He said he had completed the speech for the assembly, and, added sweetly that he'd made a fresh pot of coffee. Susan walked into the kitchen and grabbed a cup of coffee. She returned to the living room to join her husband, but, stopped first at the bottom of the stairs to yell for her kids to come downstairs.

Brian turned his head upon hearing the kids running into the living room. Susan asked the kids if they were going to give her a hug and a kiss. They walked over and hugged and kissed her and Brian. He asked his kids to finish their homework and get ready for dinner.

Gloria's cell phone rang. It was Christina, one of her best friends from school. Gloria asked Christina what was up. Christina revealed that some girls were harassing Johnny and arranging for him to show up at a place where other students were planning to humiliate him.

Christina asked Gloria to join her, in hopes of stopping the harassment. Gloria got permission from her dad, who said, "As soon as you've finished your homework, you may go."

Gloria quickly completed her homework and headed out. She told her father that Christina had arrived and that the two were headed to "The Burger Joint" where the teenagers hung out.

Christina and Gloria arrived before Johnny showed up. They got a booth and settled in. Then some other girls came and sat with them. Gloria was easily able to see the front door. She noticed Johnny as he walked in. He was carrying a lovely bouquet of flowers. He sat in a booth facing the door.

Johnny was wearing blue jeans, a red-and-white striped shirt, and white Converse athletic shoes. All Gloria could do was watch and hope she had an opportunity to tell Johnny that the scheme was a prank.

At that moment, a girl walked in and sat with Johnny. She was dressed as if she were headed to a nightclub. She wore a black, low-cut top, a black leather mini skirt, and high-heeled stilettos. She reminded Gloria of a nightclub frequenter, adorned in a lot of makeup and jewelry.

The other students were staring and waiting for what was going to happen next. Gloria looked at Johnny. She noted that he seemed embarrassed because the teens in the dining room were laughing and talking about him. The server walked up and took their order. Johnny ordered a hamburger, fries, and a Coke. The girl ordered a burger with everything on it, fries, and lemonade.

Soon the waitress brought their meals. When they finished eating, they got up from their booth. Johnny paid for the meal and they left. Gloria noticed that the girl then returned. She went to a table where some guys were eating.

One guy immediately reached into his jacket pocket. He pulled out some folded cash and handed it to the girl. She then turned and walked out of the restaurant.

Gloria managed to get up from her table where she'd watched the sickening interactions. "I hope you guys are satisfied and enjoyed the show!"

Gloria told Christina she wanted to go home. Christina and Gloria were both embarrassed about how everyone treated Johnny and planned such an event.

Christina dropped Gloria off at her house. Gloria walked inside as she cried. She gave her dad a hug and told him what she'd witnessed. Then, in rage, she ran upstairs to her bed. She needed a good cry, a cry of disappointment. A cry of despair for Johnny.

Susan followed Gloria to her bedroom. She knocked on the door and asked to come in. After a couple of hours, Susan came back downstairs and shared the details with Brian. They sat together in disbelief.

As bedtime approached, Brian knocked on Patrick's door. He slowly opened the door and told his son good-night. Then he knocked on Gloria's door and asked if it was okay to come in. Brian kissed Gloria on the forehead, told her good night, and that he loved her very much. Then he turned off the light and closed her bedroom door. He smiled as he thought about the strength of his teens.

The next morning after everyone left for school, Brian drove to his church office to prepare paperwork and attend a staff meeting. In addition, he had several things to do to prepare for the Wednesday night Bible study.

Brian had a meeting with some of the volunteers and grilled them as to the order of service for the gathering. He needed to prepare for appointments with some of the youth after school. Brian was eager to know what happened at school, so he gathered everything and headed home to get ready for the service. He opened the front door. The kids were waiting for him. They ran over and hugged him, greeting him with smiles on their faces.

Susan greeted him at the door with a kiss and told the kids to let their father relax. He gathered his composure and asked the kids how school was. The teens jumped with excitement to see their father and they couldn't wait to tell him. Brian asked Gloria to wait for him in his office. He wanted to talk with her after a moment with Susan, who said that some students were sent to the office because of the prank they pulled regarding Johnny the night before.

Brian was relieved as well as surprised that something had been done about the incident. Gloria told him that she and Christina told the principal what happened. The principal gave the students in-school suspension.

Brian asked her about Johnny and if anything happened to him. Gloria replied and said she saw Johnny by his locker and apparently someone had placed red roses on his locker for a joke. She added that nothing else had happened that she was aware of. Brian told Gloria he was proud of her for turning the students in.

Patrick then had his moments with his dad. Brian asked his son about his day and if he knew anything else about the harassment directed toward Johnny. Patrick did not.

Patrick shared with his dad about soccer practice and his current math grade. Brian was proud of his son for doing well on his exam. He then asked Patrick about practice. Patrick shared with his dad that he made the starter line up. Brian grinned and shook his head, hugged his son, and told him that was great.

Brian asked if anything really bad happened to Johnny. Patrick said he only saw Johnny in class, and nothing really happened. Brian thanked his son and told him to get ready for a quick dinner before the upcoming youth service.

Brian walked into the kitchen and grabbed a cup of coffee. He put his arms around his sweet wife and kissed her. He told her he was headed upstairs to get ready for the youth meeting and he'd be back down soon for dinner.

After the service, several students came forward and dedicated their lives to Jesus. Brian felt good about the service and how everything went. Some students walked up afterwards and thanked him for his message. The youth leaders shook Brian's hand.

Brian walked to one of the student leaders and asked if he'd be interested in sharing a message next week. Then he asked two students and asked if they'd like to share at the flagpole. Both agreed.

Brian knew he had a busy week as he prepared for the assembly. He asked his kids to write down what they wanted to share at the assembly. Patrick and Gloria told their father how much they enjoyed the service then asked if they could stop and get some ice cream.

The foursome sat in a booth and enjoyed their ice cream. Patrick and Gloria asked their father if he had any suggestions. Brian told his kids not to worry about what to say but to write what was in their hearts. He reminded them to place their trust in the Lord and allow the Holy Spirit to guide their thoughts.

Brian knew the kids had great faith in their abilities and they knew the Lord. Brian realized that the next few days would be crucial and put strain on the family. After they finished their ice cream, he asked his family to pray over the situations they faced. Patrick led them in prayer.

The next morning, Brian began by asking the students to come in close and circle up. He wanted to make sure everyone could hear the message that was on his heart. He saw Johnny sitting on the bench.

He hoped nothing would happen, but he was wrong. A student quickly grabbed Johnny's cap, tossing it in jest back and forth to other students. Brian heard Johnny speak up, asking for his hat.

After the message, Brian walked over to Johnny. "I wish people would stop bothering me and leave me alone!" Johnny was visibly shaken. Brian told Johnny he understood and asked if Johnny wanted to join the circle.

"I'll think about it and let you know," Johnny replied.

Brian headed to the van. He then heard a ruckus and rushed to see what was happening. Johnny was hitting a student. Brian adamantly told the students to knock it off. He grabbed each teen by the arm and headed to the principal's office.

He explained that the boys had grabbed Johnny's cap and were teasingly trying to keep it from him. Brian didn't know who started the fight or what it was about.

Principal Jackson reassured him that she'd handle it. Disa-ppointment fell over Brian's face. He heard the boys blaming Johnny for the fight. He then heard the principal call Johnny over the loudspeaker.

Brian was concerned about Johnny being suspended for fighting. Brian could only pray.

CHAPTER 5: CAMPAIGN AGAINST BULLYING

*I*t was Friday morning and Brian had just arisen. He showered and shaved. He then dressed, selecting a light-blue dress shirt, gray dress slacks, and a red tie. Susan was wearing a blue dress and black, high-heeled shoes. She wanted to make a statement of support for her husband, knowing her presence with him on the stage at the assembly was very important to him. She'd requested the day off and was looking forward to a day away from the classroom.

The family met in the kitchen for breakfast. Brian then asked Susan to read his speech one last time. He wanted to make sure he didn't make any mistakes. Now it was time to load into the van and head to school.

It was just like any other day as they gathered around the flagpole with a band of students and prayed. Thirty students eagerly showed up that morning. Then, around 8:20 a.m., Brian and Susan went to the school gymnasium to prepare for the all-school assembly.

Even though Brian was nervous, he knew his wife and teens would be too. After just a few minutes, the students began strolling into the gym. Brian's time to share his heart was approaching. He glanced into the crowd and saw loyal faces —

faces of students who were the faithful attenders Wednesday nights at church and each morning around the flagpole.

Brian's teens came onto the stage to join him. Everyone settled into their seats and the large room grew ominously quiet. Principal Jackson approached the podium to introduce Brian.

Brian sprang to his feet as the crowd applauded. He thanked Mrs. Jackson, then introduced his family, and shared with the crowd that he was the new youth pastor at the Methodist Church. He then said that he wanted to share about his family's story of loss — the loss of their daughter and sister, Stephanie.

He began, "Good morning, students and faculty members. I want to share with you this morning about Stephanie, my younger daughter. Stephanie had long red hair and blue eyes. She adored her older brother, Patrick, and older sister, Gloria, whom many of you know."

"It's been almost a year today," Brian hesitated briefly in a moment of emotion. "It was late afternoon when my wife, Susan, called me in a frantic voice telling me to come home. I was stunned to hear the panic in her voice. What was going on? In my mind, of course, as a father and a dad, I was thinking the worst, the absolute worst."

"My mind was racing! Did our house get broken into? Was there an accident? I never imagined what the problem could be; however, I knew I had to get home as fast as I could."

"I got home and found my wife crying. She explained that Stephanie had locked herself in her room earlier. Susan said she had hollered at Stephanie and asked her to open the bedroom door. There was no response. Susan relayed how her worst fears were swimming in her head. She then grabbed the bedroom key and opened the door."

"Susan then told me that she saw Stephanie lying on her bed. I noticed that Susan was trying to catch her breath as she tried to tell me what she saw at that moment. She saw our daughter's lifeless and still body. Next to her was an empty pill bottle. Pills were scattered on the floor. Susan relayed to me that her heart was beating faster than ever, just as my heart is doing now as I share with you teens."

"My wife then rushed over to Stephanie, shaking her and yelling at her. After no response from Stephanie, Susan yanked her phone out of her pants pocket and struggled in panic to call 911. With the dispatcher on the phone, Susan revealed what was going on. At that point, Susan called me."

"I got home just as the emergency personnel were arriving. I was praying diligently, asking God not to let my baby die," Brian continued.

"The police arrived with EMTs, who immediately rushed into the bedroom with their equipment and a stretcher. One minute later when the officer came out, I could tell by his facial expressions that our nightmare was a reality. It was too late. Our Stephanie was gone."

"The officer asked if we knew what happened to our daughter. He explained to us that he'd found a note on her desk.

He asked me if I'd like to go with him to retrieve the note. I walked upstairs with the officer, not knowing if my weak knees could even take me to the top of the stairway, much less into my daughter's room." Brian paused for a moment as his eyes glazed over the silent crowd.

"I picked up the note, still believing that maybe the scene was not real; that maybe it was just a bad dream and that I would wake up soon. It was important that Susan and I read the note together, so the officer and I went back downstairs where Susan was waiting with the other EMTs and another officer."

"My daughter wrote that she was sorry. She told us that she loved us. She said she loved her brother and sister very much. Then," Brian added hesitantly, "she added the reason she took her life. You see, the reason was in writing. The reason my daughter was gone. The reason she believed her life had no purpose. The reason she felt unworthy." Brian hesitated a brief moment as he tried to regain his composure.

"My precious daughter's words revealed that she was tired of the other kids teasing her, calling her names, and making fun of her. She said that she felt like she couldn't fight back. She believed that trying to defend herself or retaliate would just make matters worse. She wrote that she didn't want to live anymore. She said no one cared. She said she had no hope. No one wanted to be her friend. So, she just decided to take her own life."

As if the room were not quiet and still enough already, a deafening silence hung in the rafters. No one spoke and no one moved. It was obvious that Pastor Brian's testimony had meant something powerful to the students. Brian noticed that the administration staff and the teachers were also visibly moved. Many were wiping tears from their eyes. It was as if a huge cloud of emotion had entered the room and fell heavily on everyone.

"We were numb, Susan and me. We were stunned. We were sad. We were beyond sad. We just sat, almost frozen to the sofa and to each other."

"The detective filled out the incident report and asked if we needed anyone to talk to. I told him that I would notify our senior pastor at church and that it was time to pick up our son and other daughter from their after-school practice sessions. I knew that I could lean on our pastor and that he'd be there for us.

"And, I knew I'd need a lot of supernatural strength from God to share the devastating news with my teens. My physical strength was leaving me; I felt weak all over. My arms and legs began to shake. I needed to sit down so that I wouldn't fall."

"After everyone left, I called a neighbor to come over and sit with Susan. She came. We explained why we needed her presence at that moment. She'd known us for years and she'd been a dear confidant to Susan. She was like family already. The two women began to cry together."

"I was glad that Susan would not be alone while I went to pick up our kids from practice early. I was a mess, yet, I was trying to hold it together until both Patrick and Gloria were with me. I then shared with them that we had some sad news. The ride home was difficult; but, they were patient, knowing we needed to be with their mom before I talked in detail."

"Gloria was the first to realize that the news was indeed terrible. I burst into tears as we walked into our front door. Susan and our neighbor were waiting. Our neighbor slipped out quietly, knowing we needed some family time. Gloria immediately asked where Stephanie was. She knew our tears were real."

"We want you to know that Stephanie is gone, I told my teens. She died this afternoon. She took her own life. The EMTs came. They took her, I told them. I then sensed a huge emotional darkness in the room with us."

"The grief was truly unbearable. My other two children were beyond devastated. They loved their little sister. The three were always close and had great fun together."

"I then asked my teens if they had any idea or had seen any hints that their younger sister was being picked on at school. My teens were crying uncontrollably. We all just cried for a few minutes. It was difficult for us to even catch our breath at times; but, I knew my kids would share with us if they knew anything that could help us understand."

"Gloria and Patrick looked at each other through their sobbing. Gloria said she did indeed know that her sister was being bullied at school. I asked Gloria why she'd not shared this information with us, her very own parents, or why she'd not shared in confidence with another adult whom she could trust."

"Gloria told us that she had promised Stephanie she wouldn't say anything. Of course, I was hurt and confused that my girls had not spoken up. As any parent, I would have wanted to know that my child was being harassed or bullied."

"As any parent or school leader, I would have taken immediate action to help. Please understand this today, students. The adults in your lives want to help.

"We want to listen. We truly care. There may be times when you don't think we care, but we do. We were once teenagers just like you guys." Brian paused a bit to let his sentiments sink in with the students.

"I then shared with my teens that we, their mom and I, wish we had seen the signs that Stephanie was troubled. And, I told them of the note that she left behind. It was indeed the toughest afternoon and evening and night that we've ever had. We did not and could not sleep that night.

"I wish you young people could understand that the feeling of *'I wish I could have done something'* is real and heavy. Very heavy. Even today, this feeling weighs heavily on the four of us."

"We then had to call our families and close friends. The next few days were very difficult and busy. They went by in a blur. We could barely focus on anything or take time to eat. Our grief was more than we could bear, it seemed. We were grateful to have support from our church family. Church is important. Equally important is having a support group. For us, these were already a part of our lives. Our church came alongside us to support us."

"So, after a few months, and realizing we needed a change, we prayed and asked God to lead us. We knew that if we trusted Him, He would lead us from pain to victory."

"Here we are now in Millsville. We are now a part of you. We are all a part of each other. We are all responsible for each other. We are not little islands, drifting through life. We are a body of human beings, doing life together. We need each other. Please, students, do not think you are alone. There is always someone who will listen."

"Thank you for allowing me to share with you. Now I want to ask Patrick and Gloria to come to the podium and talk with you guys about the campaign that we are starting. It's very important that we look at ways in which we can make a difference. It's our responsibility to make a difference — here at school, at home, in our neighborhoods, wherever we go."

Patrick began his speech first. "We want to make our school safe from violence and bullying. I hope everyone will join us in the fight and put an end to the teasing, bullying, and name-calling." He shared a heartfelt message to encourage everyone and give the students something to think about. His message that he left with the students was "Let's take the time to pray for each other! We are a community and each one of our lives matter!"

Then Patrick said, "I think we should take the time to pray for our classmates because of the enemy that walks the hallways and seeks out the ones who are weak. It's up to all of us to stop the school violence and end the teasing, name-calling, and the bullying before someone gets hurt."

Patrick was convincing as he continued. "We need to watch out for the kids who sit alone in the school cafeterias, the ones who have no friends to turn to, and anyone else who might be teased because of their looks or clothes, or whatever."

Patrick added, "The enemy is Satan and the only way to destroy the enemy is by showing love and compassion toward each other and praying for each other. The power of both prayer and love can silence the enemy.

"Instead of finding ways to spread hate and violence, let's try to spread love in the hallways by standing up for those who are unable to defend themselves from the teasing and harassment and ugly words. Let's take the time to pray each day for our classmates who are in schools."

After Patrick spoke, Gloria walked boldly to the podium and asked the students these five questions: "How can we make a difference in our lives? What can we do to change the way we view each other? How can we stand up for those who are easy prey to be picked on by bullies?

"How can we silence the name-callers, the teasers, and anyone else who may be a threat to someone else? How can we spread love to someone who has no friends or someone who feels alone?"

"I agree with my brother. We should spread love and treat everyone as equal. We must work together to make this school a safe place. Let's all try to get along with each other. Together, we can make a difference and be someone's friend!

"You guys, everyone needs a friend, no matter who they are. If someone has problems with their homework or their grades, let's try to tutor them so they can be successful and feel good about themselves," she continued.

"Let's create a strong community. It's important to build a community around us. And, we don't need to use violence to solve our problems. We just need each other. We must pull together and encourage each other. Violence is not the answer. I lost my sister because of teasing and bullying, and I don't want to lose my friends that way too. We have a school counselor whom we can talk to and we have our parents. Most importantly, we have each other to turn to for help and support."

After Gloria finished talking, everyone stood and applauded. Brian didn't believe there was a single dry eye in the gym. Even Brian and Susan cried. Brian then looked over to his wife and asked her if she'd like to say something.

Susan walked over to her daughter, gave her a kiss on the forehead, and embraced her with a warm hug. She told her that she was very proud of her. Then she walked to the podium, looked at her children and smiled. Boldly and confidently, she then turned, stood tall, and faced the crowd.

Susan began, as she placed her hands and forearms on the edges of the podium, "I have never been as proud of my children as I am standing here today. That day when I got home from school, I felt something was wrong, but I didn't know what it was until I saw Stephanie's bedroom door closed and locked. I knocked and no one answered. Brian and I believe in our children and trust them enough, so we choose to give them their privacy."

"I never knew my beautiful little girl would take her own life. I thought we were a pretty close family. We ate together, had family game night, watched television as a family, and had Bible study together," Susan paused, as if reflecting on the memories. "And, we often enjoyed going to visit the kids' grandparents, who loved them so much."

"The children usually did their homework first thing when they got home. I just thought Stephanie was up in her room, quietly doing her homework. She never seemed to mind doing homework and always wanted to complete it before dinner time."

"When Stephanie was ten, she was in the school play as a princess. When she was eleven, she wanted to play the clarinet. For her twelfth birthday party, we had several of her friends come over and she gave a recital. She was pretty good for her age. She wanted to take ballet and we told her that she could take lessons after school. She was quite excited about ballet."

"I am here this morning, not as your teacher, but as a mother who has lost a precious child. I will stand up and take a stand. We must put an end to the teasing, name-calling, and the bullying.

We are asking each of you to help—help be a friend. Watch out for your fellow classmates. Keep an eye on your friends. Notice who needs an extra hand, a warm smile, or a kind word. Not only is it great to notice people who may have a need; but, it's equally important for those people to feel noticed. Think about that. When we truly reach out to help others, we, too, are blessed."

Susan paused. "I would like to thank my husband, my children, and this school for your support, and for the thoughts of our little girl who was taken from us at such a young age."

"I would also like to thank Mrs. Jackson for allowing us to share with you. I hope you will join the fight to stop bullying in the school. I would like to turn this over to Mrs. Jackson now."

Mrs. Jackson stood to her feet and began applauding. Everyone else did too. Brian was so very proud of his wife and her strength. And, he felt so very blessed to hear the sound of applause resonating from the rafters.

Mrs. Jackson walked to the podium and said, "Attention students. It's 9:45 a.m. We have fifteen minutes before class starts. If anyone has any questions, please come forward." Mrs. Jackson then explained to the students that there was information the students could pick up before they left for class.

Brian walked over and gave Susan a big hug. His teens did the same. Then Gloria and Patrick put their arms around Brian and hugged him too.

Brian looked over to Susan and glanced over at the information table. Sadly, only a few students picked up the information that was displayed. He was surprised that only ten students asked them questions.

Brian thanked Mrs. Jackson for letting them share with the students. She said she'd talk with the school board to see if they could implement the campaign that the children had put together. She also asked if Brian and his family could attend. He responded, "Yes. Susan, the children, and I will be at the board meeting."

Brian made a trip to the van to load up the materials and props. Then, he quickly went back into the school just to make sure he'd gotten everything. There was Johnny, sheepishly lingering behind the other students who had headed off to class.

Johnny came over to Brian and extended a manly grip, then a hug. Johnny asked Brian if he truly believed the campaign to end bullying would work.

Brian responded, "We will try our best to get this going, and we are asking God for His help. But, as you may have figured already, we first have to get permission from the school board."

This was the first time Brian had seen Johnny smile or even say a word to him. Johnny even asked if he could talk to him sometime. Brian eagerly replied, "Sure. I'll check my schedule and see when I can fit you in."

"That will be fine," said Johnny as he adjusted his backpack on his right shoulder, grinned shyly, and headed to class.

Brian started to head back to the car and felt good about his time at the podium as well as his brief conversation with Johnny. Brian believed that he was actually reaching Johnny. He and Susan were planning to spend the remainder of the day together. Susan was pleased to know that a well-respected and popular substitute teacher would be covering her history classes that day.

Brian got in the van and told Susan about the encounter with Johnny. Then, Brian asked Susan if they could quickly stop by the office before selecting a place for their lunch date.

Driving to the office, Brian realized that he liked the idea of popping into the office mid-morning after such a productive start to his day. Before heading to his office for a few minutes, he stopped first to speak with the church secretary, Mrs. Reginia Goodwin. It dawned on him for the first time to ask her if she happened to be related to Johnny Goodwin. Yes, she replied. Johnny was her grandson.

Brian was elated inside, yet, maintained a casual demeanor. He asked Mrs. Goodwin to see if he had a slot open so he could schedule an appointment with Johnny.

The best spot was Friday at 4 p.m. Brian asked Mrs. Goodwin to please call Johnny and schedule an appointment with him. She said she would.

Brian walked outside, got into the van and shared with Susan the good news. In just a few days, Brian would be face-to-face with Johnny.

The two decided to head to a Mexican restaurant, South of the Border. The restaurant was full, but, they finally were seated and ordered. The waitress looked at Susan. "You're my son's history teacher. I'm Sally Goodwin, Johnny's mother."

Susan said, "Yes, I am, and this is my husband, Brian."

About midway through their meal, Brian and Susan noticed a man walk into the restaurant. He was wearing a red baseball cap, blue denim short-sleeved shirt, and blue jeans. Brian noticed that the guy seemed to be a bit drunk.

The man sat at the bar. Soon he was talking loudly and arguing with the waitress. She then walked over to another of her tables, and then, to the table where Brian and Susan were. She asked if Susan wanted any coffee or dessert.

Susan asked softly about the man at the bar. The waitress replied that he was her husband, Bill, and that he was home for the weekend because he drives a truck during the week.

Later in the afternoon, Brian went to pick up his teens. He knew his kids had probably had a long and taxing day. Patrick joined Brian in the front and immediately pulled out his tablet to watch a video game.

Brian then glanced in the rearview mirror. He saw Gloria reading. He was proud of his teens. He knew Susan was also. He planned to tell them so at the dinner table that evening.

Nightfall came quickly and the end of another busy day had slipped away.

CHAPTER 6: A TIME FOR BONDING

Brian was curious to learn how his teens were reflecting on the assembly. He was quite proud of the anti-bullying campaign they had successfully launched.

Brian headed upstairs to talk with his children as they prepared for bed. He first knocked on Gloria's bedroom door. She replied quickly, asking her dad to come in.

Brian walked in and noticed an illustration on her desk. He asked her what she was drawing. Gloria was painting a picture of a horse with Stephanie riding it. Brian was amazed at how talented Gloria was. He kissed her on her forehead and said that the drawing looked very realistic. And, he told her how proud he was of the speech she'd made. He reminded Gloria how God wanted to use her to make a difference at the high school.

Gloria asked her father if he could stay for a while. They sat on the bed as she talked of Stephanie and how much she missed her. Gloria told her father of some activities she and Stephanie had done together — certainly things that memories are made of.

Brian told her it was okay to remember the good times they had with Stephanie. Then Brian asked her if she would be interested in spending the next day together as a daddy-daughter day. Gloria was all in favor of spending time with her dad. Brian said he'd plan a fun day with surprises. He then hugged his teen and kissed her good night.

Brian casually walked to Patrick's bedroom and knocked on his door. Patrick invited his dad in. The teen was lost in concentration, playing a video game. He asked his father if he wanted anything in particular. Brian shared that he wanted to talk. Brian stressed to Patrick that he was certainly proud of the message Patrick had shared from the podium.

Patrick thanked his dad for the compliment and went back to his game. Brian asked Patrick to please shut off the game so the two could talk. Patrick reluctantly turned off the game and pushed aside his tablet. Brian was eager to ask his son if he were interested in going camping or fishing or playing a round of golf the following weekend.

Patrick agreed that spending time with his dad was indeed something he wanted. Then, Brian asked his son about his thoughts regarding the assembly. Did the students get anything from the message? Patrick believed some students responded very well. Patrick thought that maybe the interested students could be champions for the anti-bullying cause. He'd heard some students talking about possibly planning a revival after school.

Brian mentioned to his son that it would be great if there were a student-led revival in the near future. Brian turned to head out of his son's room and paused to tell Patrick that he was looking forward to spending weekend time with him.

The next morning Gloria was already for her father-daughter day and eager to find out what they would do together. Brian was downstairs making coffee and Susan was getting breakfast ready. Susan asked Brian if he knew what he was planning to do with Gloria that day. Brian whispered that he was considering horseback riding or eating out. He asked Susan her thoughts.

Susan thought that horseback riding was fine, but she also suggested possibly going to a bookstore to find a good book. She also suggested bowling, playing miniature golf, or catching a movie. Brian thanked Susan for the suggestions and said he'd come up with something soon so as to surprise Gloria. His teen was ready, so the two headed out the front door as Gloria pondered what activity they'd be doing first.

Brian eagerly told her that their first stop was to the horse ranch in the country to go horseback riding. Gloria was surprised and excited; she was also very curious as to what great activities would follow. Brian had planned bowling, miniature golf, and a movie, and, possibly time for the bookstore.

After they finished riding, they headed to the bowling alley. Brian purposely didn't bowl his best; he wanted to let his daughter's bowling skills outshine his. Gloria said she still had some energy left, so, miniature golf was next on the agenda. Brian still wanted to stop by the bookstore. While Gloria browsed, Brian slipped next door to a jewelry store. He wanted a perfect gift for his daughter to remind them of this perfect date.

Brian returned to the bookstore. Gloria decided on a book and they left, hoping to find something good to eat. As they waited for their food order, Brian handed a glittery jewelry box across the table to his daughter. She opened the box gently, revealing a beautiful necklace. Gloria looked up, smiling and with tears in her eyes as she thanked her dad for the lovely gift.

Now it was time for the movie, their last event for the day. As they were leaving the restaurant, arm in arm, Gloria looked up at her dad to tell him she loved him. At that moment, Brian glanced past Gloria and thought he saw Johnny walking into the gun store with his father. Brian wasn't sure it was Johnny, so, he asked Gloria to take a look. She agreed that the young man was Johnny. She reassured her dad that there were other items for sale in the store besides firearms and ammo. Gloria said she'd seen Johnny going into the same store before. The store sold hobby and art supplies and other things that she and Patrick had purchased in the past. Brian asked Gloria if they could take a quick detour and head to the store were Johnny and his dad were.

They headed to the art supplies. Brian noticed Bill by the camping area and hoped to engage Bill in a conversation. Brian introduced himself and his daughter. Bill seemed a bit perplexed and asked if he knew Brian. The two had discussed camping recently at the restaurant, Brian recalled. They shared how Bill and Johnny were planning a trip.

It was a cordial encounter and just the brief face-to-face moment that Brian had hoped for. Brian then said they needed to head home. As he glanced back, Brian saw Bill and Johnny talking with a salesclerk about a gun. Brian began thinking of how he should plan a camping trip with his son.

Gloria shared with her father about how much she enjoyed the time they'd spent together. Gloria couldn't wait to finish her drawing and tell her mother about her day. At home, they shared the details of Gloria's day when Brian walked into the kitchen. Susan told Brian how much she appreciated the necklace.

Susan smiled at her husband. "This day really meant a lot to Gloria, sweetie. Thank you for spending your Saturday with our daughter and giving her a necklace to remember the day. What a sweet token of your love for her."

The next week, Patrick and his father were getting ready to go on their camping and fishing trip.

"Son, would you like to go play some golf afterwards?" Patrick asked.

"Sure, Dad. That's cool. Whatever you'd like to do."

The first stop was the gun store. Patrick stopped to purchase fishing lures while Brian selected a pocketknife for Patrick.

"How 'bout just fishing and playing some golf instead?"

"Sure, son. That's a good plan. Let's hope the fish are biting!"

As they fished, Brian gave pocketknife to his son. He was so very proud of his son and daughter. He just knew God was going to use them in a big way.

"Dad, thanks for a wonderful time and thanks for the pocketknife," Patrick said joyfully.

CHAPTER 7: HOMECOMING DANCE

The next Monday everyone at school was diligently preparing for the homecoming game and dance. Patrick had recently turned sixteen and had received his driver license. He was eager to drive his date to the festivities.

The girls were trying to decide who would run for homecoming queen. A few popular couples were running as candidates for the homecoming court — Patricia Miller and Alan Johanston, Alysia Sanders and Patrick Hanson, Tina Simson and George Dillings, Christina Hopkins and Carl Fitzgerald, and Susan Conway and Fred Carlson. One couple would be crowned king and queen; the others would be members of the court.

The school was abuzz regarding all the events of a big Wildcats homecoming. The candidates designed and posted signs around the school in hopes of soliciting enough votes to win as king and queen. All the students decorated their lockers in their school colors of blue and gold to show their support for the football team and their school. The festivities made everyone feel excited about the game and the big weekend.

Johnny was feeling bold enough to try to find a date. He asked several girls to the dance, but there were no takers. So, he finally decided to ask Patricia. She politely shared with Johnny that she was going with Alan Johanston, the captain of the football team.

Johnny turned and walked off as he politely said in a whisper that it was fine. He wanted to go to the dance, and he wanted to approach other girls, but, they turned and walked away from him, some acting a bit rudely. Johnny retreated to his locker. It was time to prepare for art class.

During homecoming week, the students dressed in costumes and enjoyed various activities; however, the Friday before the game, they all planned to dress in blue and gold. Monday was Wear Blue Jeans Day, so everyone wore jeans to school. Tuesday was 50's and 60's Day. Even the teachers and staff looked as if they were playing a role in an Elvis Presley movie. Wednesday was Safari Adventure Day. On Thursday, the students dressed up like the Old West. Friday, of course, was Wildcats Day.

After school on Monday, the student council members hung a "Go Wildcats!" sign above the front doors of the school. Other students worked to decorate the gymnasium for the homecoming dance. Other groups of students worked on the school floats for the parade. The school band practiced many hours all week for both the parade and the homecoming game.

So far this fall the home team had won two games and had only lost one. This Friday they would play against the Cartersville Cougars. So, naturally, they were practicing well and hoping for a big win. The cheerleaders too were busy getting their routines perfect and practicing their jumps.

This year the students voted to allow the girls to ask the guys to the dance. And, the theme they voted on was Jungle Safari. The students designed safari passes for those who wanted to attend the dance. Each pass cost five dollars, money that would go into the senior class fund for end of year events.

The guys wore their passes around their necks every day until the dance. It helped the girls know who had already been asked to the dance. And, the ballot boxes were set up for the voting of the homecoming king and queen and their court.

On Friday, everyone showed up for the parade and cheered for their class float. The judges determined that the sophomore class had the best float and awarded first place to the sophomores. The freshman took third place and the junior class took fourth place. The seniors got second place.

The homecoming parade was a huge success. All the floats boasted of a lot of student participation — much hard work and long and late hours. Brian was very proud of the student body and the efforts they gave to float design, construction, and teamwork. The band and majorettes did a great job too, building team spirit in the onlookers.

The football game proved to be quite exciting. It was a close game, but the Wildcats lost by a field goal. The final score was 24-27. The Wildcats almost had another touchdown and could have won the game, but it was intercepted with less than two minutes left. Brian was cheering in the stands and he believed his team would win.

The Cougars proved themselves as the winners. After all, they had now won four straight games. Brian was pleased that there were no injuries to the players. And, he thought Alan Johanston did an excellent job as quarterback. Likewise, Carl Fitzgerald did a great job as running back. He scored one touchdown during the first quarter; Fred Carlson, the wide receiver, scored two touchdowns in the third quarter. The kicker, George Dillings, scored a field goal in the fourth quarter.

The school called and asked if Susan and Brian would be interested in helping out at the dance. They agreed to help out and serve as chaperones. Tom Rawlings arrived to pick up Gloria for the dance and Susan made them pose for pictures before they left.

Gloria wore a long pink dress with a white sash around her waist. Her long hair was pulled back with a pink satin ribbon. Tom wore a sharp-looking white tuxedo with a black bowtie and cummerbund. Tom pinned a white corsage on Gloria's dress and told her how beautiful she looked. Patrick was getting ready to leave when his mother stopped him. She wanted to get a picture. The three teens then left for the dance.

The dance decorations turned out to be quite professional looking. The biggest surprise was the wooden rope bridge for the couples to walk across. The band played all evening, and the couples danced and laughed. Susan and Brian stood to the side and commented on the formal attire that the teens were wearing.

Alysia looked very nice in her yellow dress. Patricia wore a long, red formal. Tina had selected a purple dress with a lace overlay. Susan wore a short blue dress. And, a teal-colored dress was perfect on Christina.

The guys had tried their best to coordinate with their dates. Brian and Susan commented how cute the couples looked in matching colors. They helped serve refreshments and also kept a close eye on the punch bowl, ensuring that no one added anything to it.

A few parents stood outside to make sure no one brought drinks inside. Then Mrs. Jackson came forward to announce the homecoming court, beginning with the fourth runners up — Tina Simson and George Dillings. The third runner-up team was Susan Conway and Fred Carlson. The second runners-up were Christina Hopkins and Carl Fitzgerald. The first runner-up couple was Alysia Sanders and Patrick Hanson.

After a drumroll from the band, the king and queen were announced. Patricia and Alan were this year's royal couple. Brian and his family had already surmised that Patricia and Alan would get the top spots on the court.

The band started back up and the dance action began again. Brian estimated that approximately 500 students had showed up. Everyone was pretty tired, yet, it seemed all the students were having a good time. Brian and Susan walked over to the photo area for a picture. The set consisted of a bamboo hut and a primitive-looking wooden bench. Susan sat gingerly on the bench while Brian stood behind her with his right hand on her shoulder.

Brian noticed that a few of the students didn't have dates or maybe they just didn't feel like dancing. Brian walked over to see if they were enjoying the dance and having fun. They said yes and confirmed that their dates were in the restrooms. Brian said with a fatherly grin, "Okay, I just wanted to make sure." He also noticed a few girls sitting by themselves around a table.

Brian and Susan really had a great time when they had a chance to dance together. Brian had forgotten how much he enjoyed dancing with his wife. After the song ended, they paused on the dance floor and all the students began to clap for them. Brian thought that maybe his own teens would be embarrassed to see their parents on the dance floor, but, instead they applauded too.

Tina Simson, George Dillings, Susan Conway and Fred Carlson were standing around, discussing the after-party. Tina walked over to Gloria to see if Gloria wanted to attend.

"Tina, my escort, Tom Rawlings, will be taking me home after the dance."

"Okay. I understand it's going to be a great party."

Christina and Carl Fitzgerald seemed to overhear and so they walked over to Gloria to ask what they were talking about. Gloria explained to Christina that it was about the after-party. Gloria asked Christina and Carl if they planned to attend and where the party was going to be held.

Carl responded, "I overheard from Susan Conway that it was going to be at Fred Carlson's house."

Patricia Miller and Alan Johanston headed to Tina and George where they were getting punch. Alan asked George if they were going to the party. George said they would attend.

Alan noticed Johnny sitting by himself since no one would dance with him. Alan started to laugh as he thought how funny it would be if he walked over to a girl who came by herself and get her to ask Johnny for a dance. George didn't think the joke was funny. He asked Alan not to do it. George told Alan he would ask Tina if she could talk to one of the girls.

Tina spoke to one of the girls, Barbara Holt, who hadn't come with a date and she agreed to dance with Johnny. Barbara walked over to Johnny and asked him to dance. She was wearing glasses, had reddish short hair, and had on a purple dress. Johnny was excited since this was the last dance of the night and he'd get a chance to dance with someone.

Patrick asked his dad if he could go to the after-party with Alysia. Patrick promised that they would be home around midnight.

"Patrick be sure to be home right after the party," Brian admonished his son. Patrick agreed and he left with Alysia.

Gloria left with her date as she said to her dad, "Tom asked me to go with him to the party."

Brian said, "Just be sure to be home around midnight."

A group of students headed to Fred Carlson's house. At the party, Patrick noticed a few students smoking marijuana. Couples were making out on the couches. A few couples were dancing.

Carl walked over to Patrick and asked if he'd like to smoke marijuana. Patrick declined and told Carl he wasn't interested. Patrick placed his arms around Alysia and walked off. Alysia looked at Patrick and asked if he'd like to make out on the couch. Patrick agreed and they walked to the couch where he started kissing Alysia.

Carl approached Patrick and shared a plan to play a joke on Johnny at school Monday. Carl wanted to place a small bag of marijuana in Johnny's locker after school. Patrick told Carl that he shouldn't take the risk of getting caught. And, it would be unfair if Johnny got in trouble from being set up.

Patrick noticed it was getting close to midnight and reminded Alysia he needed to take her home. They walked up to her front door. Patrick kissed her goodnight and headed home. Patrick arrived just in time to witness Tom kissing Gloria goodnight. Patrick went inside. Gloria stayed outside talking with Tom. Brian was waiting on the couch for the teens to come home. Brian asked Patrick about the after-party. He explained that nothing much happened. Brian noticed Gloria was still outside talking to Tom, so he asked her to come inside.

The next day was rainy so everyone stayed inside. Gloria worked on her art project and Patrick did homework. Brian finished his message and turned on the weather, which called for rain most of the weekend. Brian was grateful that the students' parade floats had not been ruined by rain.

Patrick completed his homework. Gloria was still working on her art project when her cell phone rang. It was Tom. He asked Gloria if she would like to get out of the house, go to a movie, and then go out for dinner. Gloria told her parents that Tom was taking her out. Brian asked her to please return home no later than 11 p.m.

Susan helped Gloria select an outfit for her date. After Susan found something for Gloria to wear, she talked with her daughter for a while and then left the room and headed back downstairs. The rain had stopped. It was clear outside when the doorbell rang. There stood Tom holding a bouquet of flowers for Gloria. Susan and Brian met him at the door. Susan took the flowers and placed them in a vase with water.

"Tom, come on inside," Brian requested as Susan stepped aside. "Gloria's almost ready."

Susan called to Gloria to let her know Tom was downstairs waiting. Tom saw Gloria on the stairs and said with a grin, "Gloria, you look beautiful and I brought you some flowers."

Patrick got on his phone and asked Alysia out on a date. He shared with his dad that he was taking Alysia out to eat. After Patrick was ready, he asked his dad for the car keys. He wore a red-striped shirt and a nice pair of blue jeans. He arrived to pick up Alysia, who was wearing a casual red dress. Her parents asked when they'd return. Patrick needed to be home before 11 p.m., so he thought they'd be back around 10:45 p.m.

Patrick kept his promise and got her home before 11 p.m. He headed upstairs for bed. He thought of what had happened at the after-party the night before. He was worried about telling his dad the truth. Patrick thought maybe Carl was joking and everything would be fine. Patrick was afraid to get Carl suspended from school if he said anything so he kept rehearsing in his mind, "Should I say something to Johnny at school Monday? Will Johnny be arrested or get suspended if Carl did place the marijuana in his locker?"

Patrick tossed and turned all night about not telling his dad the truth. He decided not to say anything because he felt Carl wasn't serious. Patrick decided that the possibility of such a prank wasn't really serious enough to mention. So, he kept silent.

Chapter 8: Surrender and Revival

***M**onday morning, Pastor Brian noticed that more students were standing around the flagpole than usual. He guessed that maybe sixty students had gathered.

George Dillings walked over to Johnny at the bench and asked if Johnny would like to join them. Johnny said, "Maybe tomorrow. I'll think about it."

George then shared with Brian that Johnny would think about joining in the next day. Brian had hoped this would be the day that Johnny would join the others and feel welcomed.

After the prayer service, Brian approached Johnny and asked if he got his message to meet Friday around 4 p.m. in Brian's office. Johnny said sheepishly, "I'll be there at your office."

"I'll be looking forward to talking with you," Brian replied. He didn't realize how depressed Johnny was that day; but, Brian knew something was really bothering Johnny. Brian just didn't know what it was.

Brian stopped by Jim Fannigan's office for a moment to tell him he was making some progress with Johnny. Brian shared how he sensed that Johnny seemed very discouraged. Brian suggested that the two of them keep a close eye on Johnny.

Brian left Mr. Fannigan's office and headed down the hallway. All the students were getting ready for class, Brian noticed that Johnny was speaking with Patricia Miller, but she just ignored him and walked off. Brian walked over to Patricia and asked her if everything was okay.

"Yes, but Johnny asked me to go to a movie." Patricia politely declined and mentioned to Johnny she already had a date with the football captain, Alan Johanston. Brian told her to have a great day at school and he left.

Brian noticed that Johnny was feeling down and hurt. He also saw some other students standing by their lockers, laughing and talking about Johnny. Brian could hear just snippets of what they were saying. One boy said somewhat rudely, "There's Johnny, asking Patricia out again."

A girl replied, "Doesn't Johnny realize that Patricia doesn't like him and she's just trying to be nice?" Brian overheard another girl talking to a group of girls. She said, "I hope Johnny doesn't ask me out on a date." The girls nodded their heads in agreement.

The next morning was a beautiful and clear day. Brian just knew that God wanted him to share a message about giving something up and turning it over to the Lord. He admonished the students to study their hearts and dig deep, asking God what in their lives they needed to surrender.

After Brian finished his message, he noticed Johnny standing with the group. Several students walked up to the flagpole and placed several items on the ground that they wanted to surrender to the Lord. Many were kneeling and praying. Suddenly Brian saw Johnny raise a gun in the air. Johnny was looking around, with the gun poised, scanning the crowd.

At that moment, one of the students yelled out, "gun!" Brian feared the worst. Johnny yelled out, telling everyone to stay back and not come any closer. He wanted to let everyone know he'd had enough and that he was willing to shoot anyone who approached him.

Then Johnny focused his attention toward Brian and the other students. Brian knew that if he didn't act fast, something could go wrong and there could be several students injured or killed. As he took a deep breath, Brian casually walked toward Johnny.

Johnny's facial expression revealed to Brian that he was hurting. The tears began to roll down Johnny's face. Brian quickly prayed in his spirit, asking God for encouraging words.

Brian firmly spoke to the students. "Guys let's not panic," Brian admonished. "We must all remain calm. Please step back and do what I say."

Brian hoped that none of the students would rush toward Johnny in panic, causing Johnny to panic and begin shooting. Brian calmly gestured toward the gun and encouraged Johnny to slowly put it down on the ground. Silence fell over the crowd.

Johnny slowly started putting down the gun as he walked toward the flagpole. Brian instructed the students to slowly step away. As Johnny approached the flagpole next to where Brian was standing, he willingly laid down the gun next to the other items the students had placed there. Johnny turned toward Brian and looked down as he cried.

Johnny said with a shaky voice, "Pastor Brian, I just wanted to turn my gun over. I've been thinking of killing myself and anyone else that tries to stand in my way. But, I know that's wrong. Your words today made me realize that I have been wrong. But after hearing your message and George asking me to join the group, I've decided not to do this anymore."

Brian had instructed Carl Fitzgerald to run inside and let Principal Jackson know what was going on. Carl responded and took off running. Mrs. Jackson immediately sounded the emergency alert alarm. The teachers and staff quickly placed the school under lockdown. A few teachers came out to help supervise the scene at the flagpole.

Turning to the other students, Brian asked them to quietly and quickly go into the building. They seemed a bit frightened, but, did as Brian asked. Brian began to pray with Johnny.

Mrs. Jackson came out and stood to the side. She witnessed Brian with his arm around Johnny and knew that Brian had taken control of what could have been a dangerous situation. As Brian turned around to acknowledge her, she mouthed to him that she'd notified the police and that they were on the way.

Mrs. Jackson asked the math teacher, Mr. Blackford, if he could stand near the gun until the police arrived. He nodded that he would. Mrs. Jackson asked Brian and Johnny to walk with her to her office. Inside the outer office, Mrs. Jackson asked Johnny to join her secretary for just a minute and Brian and Mrs. Jackson shared a few words in her office.

Brian immediately asked that Mrs. Jackson call Johnny's parents. He wanted Mr. Fannigan to join them. She agreed and as soon as the counselor got there, they brought Johnny into the office. They talked until the police arrived.

When the police showed up they first confiscated the gun from the flagpole area. Two officers then searched Johnny's locker for anything that he may have hidden there. They discovered a small bag of marijuana, prompting them to search all the students' lockers. They found three other students hiding bags of marijuana in their lockers.

Mrs. Jackson explained to the police officer that Johnny's parents were on their way. Johnny's mother arrived first, at the same time that the officers where informing the principal of what they'd just discovered in the lockers.

Mrs. Goodwin stepped sheepishly into the principal's office. The officers and the staff gathered in the principal's office and talked for another thirty minutes. The police then took Johnny and the three other students into custody.

Mrs. Jackson called a special assembly in the gymnasium so that she could address the students regarding the morning's events. Rumors among the students were already spreading, because they'd seen the police vehicles parked out front.

The assembly time began as the students and faculty members gathered in the gym. All was quiet as Principal Jackson approached the podium.

She spoke factually, explaining that four students had been arrested because the officers found illegal substances in the students' lockers. She shared that such substances should never be brought to school, and, when situations like this occur, there will always be consequences.

Mrs. Jackson's directness with the students was perfect. Brian appreciated her words. And, he sensed that the crowd was pondering the seriousness of the situation. In his heart, he was still quite worried about Johnny, because he'd never thought that Johnny would have been one to bring a gun to school.

Brian was pleased that his message, George's invitation to Johnny to join at the flagpole, and God's urging in Johnny's heart, resulted in Johnny surrendering the gun at the flagpole service.

The assembly was brief, and Mrs. Jackson told the students to quickly return to class. Brian climbed into the van and headed to the juvenile detention facility to see if he could help in any way. He felt compelled to speak with the detective and other juvenile offender authorities to share his side of the story regarding what all had conspired.

As Brian waited, he saw Mrs. Goodwin crying. Brian sensed that she was greatly upset and distraught. Brian said he'd do what he could to help ease the situation, but, that he couldn't promise anything. He added that he'd speak with the senior pastor at the church to see if the church could also assist in any way.

Brian shared with Johnny's mom that the church offers family crisis counseling. She responded, "Thank you, Pastor Hanson. I'll discuss it with my husband in detail when he gets back. I have spoken to him about what happened by phone, but he's on the road and won't be back for a couple of days."

"That's fine," Brian replied, hoping the family would be willing to take advantage of the services the church offered.

Then the detective came out of his office and introduced himself as Detective John Vincent. Detective Vincent said, "Pastor Hanson, would you come into my office?"

Explaining what had happened in great detail, Brian added that Johnny never fired a shot, nor seemed as if he truly had plans to fire the gun. Brian explained that Johnny just walked up to the flagpole as other students had done, and after a little coaxing, surrendered the gun.

Brian told the detective that Johnny stated he was thinking of hurting only himself and anyone who got in his way. But, because of Pastor Brian's message, Johnny said, he'd turned in the gun. Brian also shared with Detective Vincent that before they went into the principal's office, he had prayed with Johnny.

Brian couldn't tell Detective Vincent what they prayed about because that was confidential; however, Brian could only reveal the contents of the prayer if Johnny were to give his permission. The detective took down Brian's statement, said he was free to go, and thanked him for what he had done.

Brian went to the office, talked with Ralph Cunningham, senior pastor, and explained the situation to him. Pastor Cunningham said, "I will do my best to help this family." The pastor also told Brian to take off the rest of the day.

Then, Brian picked up a hamburger and fries to take home. He arrived at 2 p.m., ate his lunch, and turned on the television. Then he went reluctantly into his study to prepare his message for Wednesday night's service. His mind was still rehearsing all the events that had transpired earlier in the day. His concerns were for Johnny.

Approximately an hour later, Brian received a call from Mrs. Jackson. Her voice was desperate as she asked Brian to come to the football field immediately. Brian was worried that something else bad had happened or it was something involving his children.

Mrs. Jackson said, "All the students are on the football field in small groups, talking and praying together." Brian asked if he could call Pastor Cunningham and all the other local churches. Mrs. Jackson agreed.

Brian share the situation with Pastor Cunningham and asked if he would call the other churches. Brian then urged Pastor Cunningham to meet him at the school football field.

Brian arrived at school and was amazed to see all the students gathered and praying. What had prompted this scenario? He was perplexed, yet greatly pleased. He shared with the principal that clergy from several churches were on their way over.

News media personnel were on the scene and setting up for a live broadcast. He quickly prayed and asked God to show up in a big way and to be glorified in this spontaneous event.

Brian searched for his family and soon found his wife and children. He asked the teens what had prompted this gathering. Patrick said, "Because of what we all said at the assembly Friday morning, Dad, and the incident that happened this morning. It was kinda sudden, Dad. Kinda spontaneous. All the students headed out to the football field where they divided into small groups to talk and pray."

Brian told his family he would meet with their pastor when he arrived. Brian was eager to see what all the pastors would choose to do to help with the impromptu event.

Walking to the pastor, Brian said, "I've never experienced anything like this before."

Pastor Cunningham agreed. "We will need to have someone stay here in case anyone needs us for support."

Brian had a quick thought that maybe after the students had prayer, maybe, just maybe revival would begin to stir. Maybe the pastors could arrange to hold an actual revival? The other pastors all agreed, as long as it was okay with the principal.

Brian noticed that staff from a pizza parlor close by began showing up. They were offering free pizzas, pizzas that had been donated. They offered to deliver as much pizza as was needed.

Brian shared with Mrs. Jackson about the gracious pizza donation and she announced to the students that free pizza was available. She then asked a pastor to lead in prayer and thank God for the food.

A band showed up later and asked if they could play music for the students. Before long, many parents began to arrive. They were curious as to what it was that was attracting such a crowd. They'd already seen publicity on the news.

Mrs. Jackson walked to the microphone and announced to the students that a band had agreed to play. She then asked if a pastor wanted to share a message.

Pastor Ralph Cunningham stepped up to her request. He walked over and began sharing a powerful message. First, he thanked the students for being bold.

"I've never before witnessed such an outpouring of the Spirit until today. We're having a revival because of you students taking the first step and gathering on the football field. I want to thank everyone for their support."

Pastor Cunningham spoke to the students for almost an hour and mentioned that pastors from other churches were in attendance. He said the pastors would be gathered up front near the podium if the students wanted to talk or pray with them. Approximately thirty pastors stationed themselves up front, to be available for the students.

The event continued until approximately 8 p.m. when everyone started to leave. The police had come to direct the traffic. Mrs. Jackson announced that classes were cancelled for the remainder of the week.

She boldly suggested that the student body and any supporters hold a tent revival service instead of the typical Wednesday night Bible study. She added that she would ask the school board to ensure it was okay to continue with the revival.

Brian and his family climbed in their van to head home. Brian talked to Susan and his children and asked if they thought continuing the revival would be a good idea. They agreed that it was a great time to continue the revival.

The revival lasted until Friday and it was remarkably successful. Approximately five hundred students attended each evening. Pastor Brian believed that almost 1,800 new salvations and rededications resulted from the revival messages. He was amazed at the responses.

Brian heard a few days later that Johnny had received a thirty-day jail sentence and a year of probation. He mentioned to Susan that he wanted to go visit Johnny to see how he was doing.

Susan was in favor of her husband's decision. She knew Brian's heart for youth was the driving force behind his desire.

"It's been almost a week now since the incident at school. I just hope he's doing all right," Brian said. He wondered what it would be like when Johnny got out of juvenile jail and returned to school. Would the students treat him the same? Would they treat him differently? Would they show kindness? Would they demonstrate Christ-likeness?

Brian decided he'd visit Johnny the following Monday. Brian wanted to let Johnny know that he truly cared about him. Brian knew God would give him the exact words to share with Johnny. After all, God loved Johnny more than Brian ever could.

CHAPTER 9: VISITING JOHNNY

Monday morning, Brian called the juvenile detention facility to get permission to visit Johnny. The clerk informed Brian that he could come to the facility, but, that there could be a wait and he'd have to complete paperwork. Brian had hoped that Johnny was okay, and he wanted Johnny to know he had a friend who cared about him.

As Brian waited in the lobby, he picked up a magazine and read, sometimes glancing curiously over the top of the magazine to observe the other people waiting there with him. Finally the desk clerk told Brian to fill out a form and take a number.

It took Brian almost half an hour to complete the tedious paperwork. Then an officer called Brian's number. Brian walked through a metal detector at the doorway to a visitation room. The room contained five small booths, each with a glass window and a two-way phone. At that moment, Johnny slowly walked in to sit on the other side of the second window. He was surprised to see Pastor Brian on the other side of the glass.

The officer instructed Brian that he had 15 minutes to visit and he should pick up the phone to speak to Johnny. Brian adjusted the handset on his shoulder and held it there steadily, quietly asking Johnny how he was doing. Johnny said he was okay and that he was ready to get out.

Brian shared with Johnny about the spontaneous revival that had occurred at the school. Johnny told Brian, with sadness in his eyes, that he was sorry he'd even brought a gun to school in the first place. Johnny added that he was reading the Bible because he had a lot of time to lie in his bed and think.

Johnny added that the marijuana found in his locker was not his. He truly believed he had been framed and that someone else, or another student, had placed it there as a prank. Brian listened intently to Johnny's words and believed them to be true.

Johnny apologized for not making the 4 pm. meeting on Friday as they'd planned. Then, surprisingly to Brian, Johnny mentioned his Bible reading again and said he'd prayed and asked Jesus into his heart. Brian smiled and quietly told Johnny that he was proud of him. God, too, was pleased with Johnny's decision, Brian said.

Brian asked Johnny if he had any other visitors besides him.

"My mom came, but, my dad still hasn't been here yet," Johnny replied, a bit sadly.

Brian told Johnny not to worry and said, "He'll visit you when he can."

Johnny asked Brian if he knew how long Johnny would be in jail. Brian replied that he did not know, but, to hang in there and be patient. It was difficult for Brian to see Johnny in an orange sweat suit that was worn and way too large. Brian began to feel sorry for Johnny and suddenly found it difficult to keep from being emotional in front of Johnny.

Johnny was worried about what the other students would think of him now. Brian mentioned to Johnny he would talk to the principal to see if he could get his homework to him. Brian reassured Johnny that he must not worry about what the other students thought; Johnny just needed to focus on being patient and trusting God.

Brian could see that Johnny had a difficult time as he tried to refrain from crying. Brian told Johnny that Jesus loves him and forgives him for what he did. Now Johnny would need to rely on Jesus so He could help him through this situation.

Brian added reassuringly, "I will try my best to come and visit you every week."

Johnny asked Brian if he had spoken with his mother recently.

"Not recently," Brian commented. "But, I will check to make sure she's all right."

Johnny asked if Brian could have the students pray for him around the flagpole. Brian said, "I will talk to the students and tell them you would like them to pray for you."

The officer came in. It was time to end the visit. Brian said, "I will talk to you again soon and I'll be praying for you." Then Brian said goodbye to Johnny.

As Brian started to leave the visitation room, Johnny turned his head slightly away and Brian could see the tears in Johnny's eyes as he was led out. Brian really didn't want to leave; he just hoped Johnny would be fine. Brian intended to talk with the principal and see if they could manage to get Johnny's homework to him so he wouldn't miss out on his classwork. Brian also wanted to check into some programs for Johnny so that his record could possibly be exonerated. The two agreed they would meet up to talk more once Johnny was released by the juvenile judge.

The next morning Brian spoke with the students around the flagpole. He shared with them that Johnny wanted them to pray for him. Brian shared with the students that Johnny had turned his heart over to the Lord and they needed to pray for Johnny's strength and hope. Brian sensed that the students didn't really want to pray for Johnny, but, George spoke up and boldly prayed for Johnny. Then the rest of the students joined George in prayer and stood in agreement.

After the students had prayed, Brian went inside to the principal's office. He spoke with Mrs. Jackson to let her know that Johnny wanted to remain in school. She replied that she'd gather Johnny's assignments, but, that she was unsure if he could remain enrolled in school. She promised to do her best to talk with her superiors and the board about allowing Johnny to return to school once he was released from juvenile jail.

The next week Brian went to visit Johnny and told him that the students had been praying for him. He also wanted to see if Johnny had gotten his schoolwork.

"Yes, I got my classwork," Johnny stated. "I was hoping you could take it and turn it in for me?" Brian agreed to take the homework to school for Johnny. Brian asked how the Bible study was coming along.

"I've been reading the Book of John," Johnny replied.

Brian also asked Johnny if anyone else had come to visit him. Johnny replied that his mother, sister, and brother had visited the day before.

"My father still hasn't come to visit."

The youth pastor explained to Johnny not worry about his father. Brian also told Johnny that he had spoken with Mrs. Jackson, but she was unsure about him being allowed to return to school. Mrs. Jackson, however, was working on it and promised to do the best she could.

Brian encouraged Johnny to keep his hopes up, continue with his classwork, and read the Bible. Brian was really surprised how Johnny's spirit had changed since the previous visit. Brian wanted to continue to lift up Johnny's spirits and encourage the students at school to continue praying for Johnny.

Brian shared with Johnny he was trying to get him into a program after his release. He explained to Johnny that he couldn't guarantee that he could get into a program to have his record erased, but, that Brian would continue to check in with Johnny's probation officer to discuss the possibilities.

The deputy came and told Brian it was time for him to leave. Brian reminded Johnny that he'd be back next week and hoped to have some good news to tell him. The two grinned at each other as if they were lifelong friends. Brian was feeling hopeful.

The following week, Brian received a call from Johnny's probation officer who requested to schedule an appointment to discuss some juvenile programs. Brian agreed and scheduled an appointment to speak with the officer. During the meeting, the officer mentioned to Brian that he would try to make the recommendation to get Johnny into an aftercare program.

Brian said, "I will do whatever is necessary to help get Johnny into the program."

The probation officer suggested that Brian write a letter of recommendation and return in a couple of days. At home, Brian began writing the letter. He asked his senior pastor to write one too. Brian spent most of the day writing the letter and working at his church office. He finally completed the letter and emailed it to Johnny's probation officer the next day.

Brian called the school principal to check on whether Johnny would be allowed back in school. Mrs. Jackson suggested that Brian attend the school board meeting and use his influence as a youth pastor to see if he could help get Johnny back in school.

Mrs. Jackson told Brian the school board would meet Thursday and she would make sure he had a few minutes on the evening's agenda. Brian began writing his speech for the meeting.

During his third visit with Johnny, Brian found out that Johnny was accepted into the aftercare program and he must complete the program to get credit for it. Brian shared with Johnny that he was diligently working to get Johnny back into school, but, that the program had to be completed first.

Brian enjoyed his visit with Johnny that morning and shared some scripture verses that were on his heart. Then, Brian asked Johnny if anyone else had come to visit him.

Johnny mentioned that Brian's senior pastor had visited last week, but, that his father had still not shown up. Brian tried to be reassuring to Johnny and said that possibly Johnny's dad was tied up with his traveling and being on the road.

Johnny also asked if any of the students had been asking about him. Brian replied that a few of the students had been asking about him. Johnny was glad to hear that, but, shared with Brian that he was feeling a bit depressed and was quite eager to get out of jail.

Just then, Johnny's mother, brother and sister arrived. The police officer told Brian it was time to leave. Brian reminded Johnny that he'd return next week, then he turned and spoke briefly with Johnny's mother. Sally dropped her head a bit as she faced Brian and quietly informed him that she was in the process of divorcing her husband, Bill, and that is the reason why he hasn't visited Johnny.

"I understand and wish you the very best," Brian stated. Brian reminded Sally that he would return for another visit and planned to be there when Johnny was released. Brian then asked her if she needed anything or if there were something he could do for the family.

"Just keep praying for us. Johnny sure does need some encouragement to stay strong."

Brian agreed. He was eager to find a solution to stop the bullying at the high school Brian added that it would take some time before they'd see positive results. He then reassured Sally that everything would work out.

Brian asked Sally if he could pray with her. Brian prayed with her and her children. He also prayed for a solution to the bullying and for school violence to end.

Johnny continued to spend most of the time in his cell reading the Bible and when he was able to go outside for sunshine and exercise. During exercise time, he talked with the other juveniles, sharing his testimony and trying to get others to join him in Bible study. Johnny was seeming to enjoy the new change in his life during the past week. He was pleased that five other guys were now joining him in Bible study.

Johnny spent time writing letters to his family. He also penned several letters to Brian to keep him informed of what was happening during his jail sentence. Johnny shared how he'd met other teens who'd been arrested about the same time of his own arrest.

Johnny took time to visit with these youth and tried to connect with them. More than anything, Johnny longed for the teens to join him in his Bible study group.

Brian made plans to be at Johnny's release hearing. Susan, Patrick, and Gloria wanted to come along also. Brian called Sally and asked her permission to buy Johnny some new clothes for the day of his release. Sally agreed, thanked Brian, and gave him Johnny's size.

The morning of Johnny's release, Brian and his teens shopped at a popular teen's store to find some new and trendy clothes for Johnny. The teens found some items they liked and that they believed Johnny would like. Brian noticed that his kids seemed to greatly enjoy selecting gifts for their new school friend.

After Brian paid for the clothes, Patrick asked his father if he could speak to Johnny after he was released. Brian had a confused look on his face, but he agreed to let Patrick talk to Johnny. The three of them drove to the juvenile detention facility. Brian's goal was to make sure they arrived on time. He wanted to show up just as the release hearing was to begin.

When they arrived, Gloria said to her dad, "I would like to hand Johnny's clothes to him." Brian thought it was a really nice gesture and he agreed to allow Gloria to give Johnny his new clothes after the hearing.

The hearing would soon begin. Brian noticed the judge, attorneys, and other personnel enter the courtroom. As the Hansons waited for their invitation to come into the courtroom,

Brian noticed Sally arriving with Johnny's brother and sister. Brian spoke with Johnny's mother and she was glad Brian took the time to visit him.

During the hearing, Brian and his family sat with Sally and her children waiting for Johnny to appear. As Johnny was led into the courtroom to appear in front of the judge, Sally reached over to Susan and squeezed her hand. They all stood up waiting to hear the Judge's opening remarks.

The hearing only lasted a few minutes. Johnny walked out of the courtroom with a grin on his face. Brian noticed that he seemed content and his countenance was calm. Now they all awaited final paperwork and the details of the probation period. The deputy handed Sally the paperwork and asked for her signature. Now they were free to go.

Brian learned that Johnny's dad had never visited Johnny in jail. Later Johnny learned from his mom that his parents were divorcing because of his dad's drinking problem, and because of the physical and emotional abuse that Sally had endured.

Sally and Brian gently embraced, and Johnny and Patrick walked over to each other. Patrick shared with Johnny that he wanted to apologize for not saying anything about the bag of marijuana. Patrick told Johnny that he spoke to the boys and they promised they'd not put the bag in Johnny's locker. At the time of the conversation with the boys, Patrick felt it wasn't necessary to say anything since the boys agreed not to execute the prank.

Johnny looked at Patrick. "You've done nothing wrong. I forgave the three boys. They are now my friends. I guess you know they were here in juvy with me. I even invited them to my Bible study group, and they came."

Gloria waited until her brother had finished talking with Johnny before approaching Johnny with the new clothes. She said that she and Patrick had selected some clothes for him.

Johnny thanked Gloria, Patrick, and Brian for the clothes and asked his mother if he could change clothes quickly in the restroom before they headed out. Johnny walked out the restroom as all eyes were upon him. He looked really nice in the new clothes. He had on a striped, blue button-up polo shirt, black slacks, and brown loafers.

Brian noticed that Sally had tears in her eyes. She proudly told her son that he looked quite handsome. Even Johnny's siblings complimented him on how nice he looked. Johnny felt attractive on the outside. More importantly, he had a new peace on the inside.

The officer at the desk called Johnny over. She handed him his small bag of personal property and asked him to look inside to see if everything was there. She explained that he would soon meet with his probation officer to go over the necessary requirements of his probation.

The probation officer then called Johnny and his mother back to the interview room. He went over the requirements and also discussed the six-month program. At the end of the meeting, he requested Brian to join them. He explained to Brian several requirements of which he needed to be aware.

The officer looked at Johnny. "Do you have any questions, and do you agree to these terms?"

"Yes, I agree. I have no questions for you at this time."

Then he asked Pastor Brian if he had any questions and if he agreed to the conditions. Brian stated affirmatively, "Yes, I agree to the conditions."

The probation officer answered a few more questions and explained details about the role of the adults so that Brian understood completely.

Lastly, the probation officer explained to Johnny that he would be required to report back to the juvenile facility in two days to meet the bus for camp. The officer explained if Johnny did not report, or if he were late, he would not be able to attend camp.

Sally reassured the officer that she would make sure Johnny would be on time.

Johnny agreed, and said, "Officer, I promise to be there on time and be ready to go."

The officer reminded Johnny that the bus would arrive at 9 a.m. He asked Johnny to please check in at 8 a.m. to have time to sign release forms and other paperwork. And, no personal items were allowed, other than one change of clothes and toiletry items. The officer reminded Johnny that he was not to bring any type of weapons, money, nor electronic devices.

Johnny asked the probation officer if he could bring his Bible to read. The officer said, "Yes, that will be fine. It is your responsibility to keep up with it." Johnny was somewhat worried because he had no idea what to expect. He was not sure what camp would be like. But, the officer reassured Johnny that they'd had a lot of success with teens at this camp in the past.

Once he completed the program, the officer continued, Johnny would go in front of a juvenile judge again. The judge would sign off on the completion of the program and Johnny's record would be exonerated. The next step would be that Johnny would continue to be on probation with supervision and counseling after his release from the program.

Johnny was informed that if he got into any trouble while at the camp, he would have to repeat the course and his record would not be erased. The goal was to stay out of trouble for the entire six months of the camp.

The morning of departure, Johnny checked his duffel bag again to make sure there was nothing in the duffel bag that he was not allowed to bring. Johnny asked the officer if he would be able to keep up with school. The officer stated that the program includes classes that he'd be able to attend.

Brian arrived at the station thirty minutes before the bus was due to depart. He wanted to visit with Johnny and Sally. Brian told Johnny to be sure to write.

"Pastor Brian, I promise to write you every week."

Brian smiled. "I'll be looking forward to your letters and will keep you informed of what's going on. I'll pray for you, son."

Brian told Johnny that he'd continue to ask the students to pray for him also. Brian reassured Johnny's family that Johnny would be fine while he was away. Brian asked them to take the time to write to Johnny and encourage him.

Brian knew in his heart that if Johnny had a collection of letters while he was at camp that he'd probably read them over and over. Sally agreed to send letters often. She too knew the value of maintaining contact with her son.

Sally wanted her son to continue to feel loved and valued, even though he would not be physically near his family and friends for several months.

Johnny walked over to his mom to kiss her good-bye. He promised that he'd write to her. He hugged his sister and extended a handshake to his brother.

Sally then noticed the bus coming down the street, so she told her son to gather up his stuff and be ready. Brian, Patrick, Gloria, and Johnny's family headed outside to wait for the bus. The expression on Johnny's face revealed that he was nervous and worried.

Johnny took a deep breath. "I guess this is it. I will miss you guys. I'll miss you a lot."

Sally began to cry. "I will miss you too, son." Sally noticed the bus was blue and had white lettering on the side that read, "Department of Juvenile Corrections."

Her stomach sank as she realized that her son was truly a part of the state's legal system. She tried to hide the tears in her eyes. Sally turned and told Johnny it was time as she hugged her son tightly. She wanted her hug to last a lifetime; however, it was time to say goodbye.

The bus pulled up to the station as Johnny turned and looked at Brian. He smiled and said goodbye. He boarded the bus, turned around, and waved goodbye to everyone.

Johnny walked down the aisle of the bus and took a seat next to the window. He waved as the driver gave the passengers instructions for their belongings and seatbelts. The bus disappeared as Brian and Johnny's other biggest fans looked on.

In his heart, Brian knew that camp would be the best growth opportunity of Johnny's life. Brian was reminded of God's promises to be with His children through the difficult times as well as the good times.

Brian thought of the Apostle Paul and how Paul never gave up on God even when in prison. Brian was reminded too of young David who battled a giant named Goliath and won.

Brian knew Johnny would be in the best of hands.

CHAPTER 10: DAILY LIFE AT CAMP CHANGE

Camp Change is located approximately 150 miles from Millsville, Missouri. It is a juvenile work camp for teen offenders who choose to attend the camp in exchange for exonerating their sentences from their legal records.

The camp's six-month program consists of counseling, work programs, structured classroom activities, sports, and other outdoor activities. The overall mission is to engage teens in rigorous activities where they can make good choices, see positive results, and hopefully change their lives for the better. Correction officers, counselors, teachers, medical personnel, and the activities director make up the staff.

When Johnny arrived at the camp, he was very nervous and hoped he'd make the right choices and perform well. He noticed some steel buildings, a lighthouse at the edge of the camp, and several other structures where he'd go for various activities.

As the bus came to a halt in front of the Annex building, the teens were asked to exit and head inside for orientation. The Annex building was the main building, located in the middle of the camp, where the introductory meetings were held. There the teens would learn camp rules and expectations.

The boys sat on one side of the assembly hall and the girls sat on the other. The director explained the rules to everyone, enforcing the primary rule of conduct. The guys were not to interact with the girls during the daytime activities and no one was permitted to leave the camp at any time. He outlined the specific times that the teens could call home, which was during a designated time on the schedule.

The staff divided the boys into three groups of thirty and the girls into three groups of thirty. Each group had two adult leaders who directed the groups throughout all activities.

During the first day of camp, the teens were given a rundown of the property and told about all the activities and where they'd be held. Attendees were assigned uniforms to wear. They were also assigned to roommates and sleeping quarters in the dorms. In addition to the Annex building, one building contained the classrooms. Other buildings housed the cafeteria, a gym, and maintenance facilities. The two tallest buildings were the dorms. One was for the guys; the other was for the girls.

Both dorms contained three floors and on each floor were fifteen rooms. One room on each floor was reserved for the staff personnel. The staff treated everyone politely, unless someone tried pushing limits or used bad language. Rules were rules, and the staff was strict when they needed to be. Each dorm room had a shower, two twin beds, two nightstands, two lamps, a desk and chair, and a locker for each person. The rooms were simple — no rugs nor curtains, only old metal blinds.

Johnny was assigned to the second floor with a roommate named Tommy Smith. Tommy had made the camp roster for being caught with illegal drugs and shoplifting. He was a red-haired ginger, super skinny, and had a bad attitude toward authority figures. Johnny was worried about how they'd get along. For several weeks, the two spent most of the time avoiding each other. One day during afternoon counseling, the counselor had the boys get to know their roommates. Johnny took the initiative to get to know Tommy and began sharing with him about his own experiences. While Tommy listened and learned a few things about Johnny, he too explained his experiences and his family to Johnny.

Tommy mentioned he was in foster care with a family of five children. Tommy added that he got hooked on drugs from a student he met at school. The student was involved in a gang called "The Cobras," and he wanted to get Tommy involved also. Tommy was later caught shoplifting as part of the initiation for gang membership. That's when he was caught with drugs. Johnny felt sorry for Tommy, yet, continued to develop a friendship with him. Johnny knew deep down inside that Tommy was no different from any other of the teens who'd gotten in trouble. Johnny decided he wanted to be a true friend to Tommy. And, Johnny was sad that he'd not been more of a friend from the beginning.

Every morning, the two roommates did their work assignments and went to class. Then they hiked across the campgrounds to attend counseling. At lunchtime, they went together to the cafeteria, then to class afterwards. For dinner, they went to the cafeteria, then back to the classrooms for a wrap-up meeting, and finally to the dorm for rollcall. The staff assigned the guys on each floor different tasks to perform each week. With each new week, the tasks rotated to a different set of guys.

Each night, a routine bed inspection was conducted. A leader sat by the exit door. Occasionally, the leaders selected well-behaved boys to help monitor through the night. Johnny didn't get much sleep because of noise and distractions. He was also preoccupied at times about his own behavior, hoping he could behave until the very end of his time at camp.

Group leaders, Jeffery Coolridge and Kent Rutledge, performed bed checks every two hours to ensure everyone was in their rooms. Either Jeffery or Kent would walk in and shine a flashlight into the rooms to make sure all were in bed.

The bed check routine went on for six months and if anyone got into a fight or got caught doing something wrong, he was sent to solitary confinement as a first offense. However, if it happened again, the teen would fail the program. Occasionally, some teens picked fights over small things such as cutting in line during mealtime, pushing each other, and or throwing objects in the dining hall. The boys who began the fights were sent to solitary confinement, located in a building next to the Annex building. There they would spend one full day in a locked room.

Some teens remained three days in solitary confinement, depending on the severity of their misbehavior. If the staff believed the teens warranted early release, then that occurred. The teens who continued to misbehave consistently or resist punishment were sent home after their parents or guardians were notified. Much was riding on staying out of trouble — namely, a clean record. Each day, the teens had time to play sports, write letters, or just relax. Some teens played soccer while others played basketball or football. Tommy asked Johnny if he'd like to join in a game of soccer. So Johnny began playing soccer with the others.

During one soccer game, Stan Rodrick began teasing and pushing Johnny, struggling to get Johnny down on the ground. Johnny's frustration grew and he was just about to hit Stan when the coach stepped in and stopped him. Rodrick received two weeks in solitary confinement for bullying. The coach looked at Johnny. "I saw what you were going to do and if I catch you again, you'll be in solitary as well. Johnny, you need to let the staff handle the situation."

Johnny and Tommy enjoyed sitting together during mealtime and became close friends. During kitchen duty one day, Tommy got into trouble with another boy and his consequence was a two-week solitary confinement. When Tommy returned to the dorm, he told Johnny that the other boy started the fight; Tommy was only trying to defend himself.

Tommy replied, "Johnny, the staff told me if it happens again, I'll be placed on another floor and I may not get to finish the program."

Johnny was listening intently. He wanted to say the right thing. "I will try and help you to stay out of trouble."

Every Sunday, the teens had the choice to attend a church service or have free time to relax and stay in their rooms. Johnny went to church every Sunday, and then returned to his room to write letters and read his Bible.

Every time the teens went outside the camp area, two guards would ensure that no one tried to leave. Every month the leaders led the boys and girls on separate hikes. The leaders divided everyone according to their dorm room floor. The hikes were usually two miles long; but, occasionally, the teens requested a five-mile hike. Johnny's first hiking trip was during Week 3. The group leaders had everyone line up early in the day.

Johnny was nervous about going on his first trip with people he didn't know. He was attentive as the teens were asked to pair up in teams of two. Johnny ended up on the fourth row. Next to him was a tall and lanky black boy named Adam Woodward. The boy behind Johnny was the muscular Stan Rodrick who'd recently been released from solitary for bullying.

Next to Johnny was an average-built guy named Anthony Ballas. Both boys were in trouble for grand theft auto. While on the hiking trip, Stan started pushing Johnny and one time he caused Johnny to trip. The leader noticed what was going on and issued Stan a verbal warning. Anthony thought the pushing and the warning were funny. He began nudging Adam in the back.

Anthony was laughing. "I think you guys need to hurry up the pace. You're slowing everyone down." When the group leader was not looking, Rodrick occasionally nudged Johnny. He then started to laugh and told Johnny to keep up.

Rodrick responded in an angry tone. "If you know better, you better keep your mouth shut or I'll have to beat you up!"

Johnny just ignored him and kept on walking. He then turned and looked over his shoulder. With a sign, he whispered in Adam's ear, "I wish these guys would stop bothering us. I'm getting tired of them nudging and pushing me!"

Adam whispered back that he agreed. "This is getting old and I'm tired of it also!"

Johnny spent a few hours writing letters to his family and his youth pastor. Once he finished a letter and had it ready to mail, the administrators would look it over and then mail it. He was not particularly fond of how they had to peruse his letters, but he understood that rules were rules.

Johnny was curious about the lighthouse. The staff said he'd have to wait until the end of the program to check it out. Johnny returned to his room and picked up his Bible, getting lost in his reading. Tommy broke the silence. He was curious about Johnny reading the Bible. He wanted to learn more. Johnny asked his leader, Jeffery, if he could start a Bible study group in his room.

"I'll check into it with the director and let you know."

True to his word, Jeffery returned later and shared that as long as studying the Bible was during Johnny's free time, Johnny was welcome to invite others. So, Johnny started a Bible study once a week for the guys on his floor. The staff soon noticed a big change in both Johnny's behavior and also that of other teens.

Johnny spent several weeks working in the kitchen and outside doing chores. He was surprised that he'd enjoyed the physical activities. He continued attending classes and completing his homework. He knew the experience he's gaining would help him land a job once he was out of the program. He also enjoyed working in the auto shop, gardening, and tending to the animals.

Johnny also enjoyed fishing yet noticed that several guys on the other floors couldn't participate because they were constantly disciplined for not doing their work. A few guys were escorted to the correction officers' quarters for trying to pick fights. Johnny was grateful that his floormates didn't exhibit the same poor behavior as the others. He hoped it was because he was reaching them through Bible study.

CHAPTER 11: ADJUSTING TO CHALLENGES AT CAMP

Each Friday afternoon, the campers eagerly awaited mail call, which was the highlight of Johnny's week. He looked forward to getting weekly letters from his mother and Pastor Brian. Sometimes, he received letters from a few of the students from school and the principal.

Johnny continued writing letters to everyone in his family and returning letters to others who had written. He shared that he was doing well, and he mentioned starting a Bible study group and playing soccer.

In addition, Johnny seemed really interested in working in the kitchen and hanging out in the carpenter shop. He designed and built a small table and a few other wooden items. He helped out some in the kitchen, preparing and cooking meals. He'd never been fond of cooking, but, as he focused on his role in the kitchen, he found that he enjoyed mealtime preparations.

The end of the second month, on a Saturday, for extra recreation, the staff took the boys out hiking and on a boat ride. Some of the guys were water skiing and tubing. While Johnny was in the boat enjoying the sunshine, Stan Rodrick pushed Johnny out of the boat and into the water. Stan was obviously still angry at Jonny for getting him in trouble with the coach.

The boat driver swung around so that Johnny could climb back into the boat. Johnny looked at Stan as he wiped lake water from his eyes. He was just about to say something when Stan gave him a dirty look.

Johnny grabbed a towel and wrapped himself in it.

"I'm sorry it was an accident. I just fell in the water," he said to the driver. Johnny quickly wanted to put the incident behind him because now it was his turn to ski.

Afterwards Tommy questioned, "Why didn't you tell the driver the truth?"

"Stan whispered in my ear that if I told, he'd really, really hurt me."

"I'm going to tell the driver the truth. If you want, come with me and we can tell him together."

Johnny nodded a bit reluctantly and walked toward the boat house on the shore. The two guys shared with the driver what had happened. As a consequence for his behavior, Stan was escorted from the recreation area and was not allowed to complete the program.

Saturday afternoon, the staff escorted Stan to the director's office to hear his side of the story. The director reviewed both sides of the story and determined that the other boys had told the truth. The group leader escorted Stan back to his room where Stan was ordered to pack his belongings. His parents were called and asked to meet him at the bus station. No one knew what the next steps would be for Stan, since he'd now failed the program.

The third month of camp had now begun. To kick off this new month, the teens met Monday morning in the Annex building to learn the routine for the month. After the meeting, the director announced that at the end of the month, if behavior overall was good, a fun dance would be held on a Saturday night. This dance would mark the first time the teens would be allowed to have fellowship together, boys with the gals.

The dance was scheduled and all the campers seemed to look forward to attending. There was an excitement in the air among the teens; they were eager to have something new to attend.

The camp leaders closely watched the crowd. The teens were not allowed to go outside together nor to sit together.

Johnny casually walked over and asked a girl to dance. She agreed. He introduced himself and learned that her name was Nancy Williams. After they'd danced a few songs, Johnny offered her a glass of punch as they visited by the snack table. He asked why she was sent to camp. Her reply was that she'd been arrested for shoplifting in a clothing store.

While they were talking and getting to know each other, Jeffery Coolridge approached the two.

"Hey, guys. I noticed you two were over here talking to each other and holding hands. You are allowed to dance with each other; we do not allow physical contact, however."

Mr. Coolridge then walked off and Johnny and Nancy returned to the dance floor.

"Nancy, I cannot believe we are not allowed to hold hands. I think he's kinda a jerk for not allowing us to hold hands." Nancy agreed and they continued dancing with each other all night until the 11 p.m. curfew. After they went back to their dorm rooms, Johnny stayed up for a while to read as he typically did. He turned off his lamp at 11:30 p.m.

The third month of camp proved to be successful overall. Now, camp was half over. The teens were eagerly anticipating the remaining half of camp — just three more months to go.

As the fourth month began, and as they did for the beginning of the third month, staff leaders held a kickoff meeting in the Annex building. Once again, the guys were seated on one side; the girls on the other. Johnny tried to see if he could find Nancy anywhere but was unable to locate her.

Camp Director Chad Willard stood before the crowd and made an announcement. He explained what was scheduled for the day and talked about upcoming projects and events. First, the teens would help out with local community service projects. They would help pick up trash, perform yard work, and paint.

It was time to begin the day's activities. The boys were then instructed to board one bus; the girls on another. Group leaders assigned boys from each dorm floor to perform specific tasks at the park. And, no one was exempt from picking up trash.

When they arrived at the park, Johnny noticed that some local police officers and a few correction officers were there. Mr. Willard stated firmly that if anyone tried to escape, the officers would place them under arrest and take them to jail.

They notified the teens that a head count would ensure that all camp attendees were back on the bus when it was time to return to camp. Everyone was then ordered off the buses and the group leaders assigned each group something to do. Johnny and Tommy were assigned to paint all the park benches.

As he painted, Johnny noticed a few girls walking on the periphery of the park. Two boys quickly decided to try to escape with the girls. The officers ran and caught the teens, who were immediately hauled off to juvenile jail.

Johnny didn't recognize any of the girls or boys who were taken into custody. His goal was to complete his project and follow the rules. He so badly longed to return home on time and as planned. Besides, he was secretly hoping that the second half of camp would pass by much more quickly than the first half.

Johnny was concerned that one of the girls may be Nancy, but none of them were. The group leaders encouraged the teens to remain focused on their projects and complete their tasks. Once they were finished with their projects, they reported to the gazebo for head count.

Johnny was certainly discouraged that two boys and two girls were now in custody for trying to run off. He didn't know their names. He whispered to Tommy, "I wonder who they are, because I noticed everyone from our group is still here."

Tommy looked over at Johnny. "Yes, I noticed that too. I'm glad. This is a rough camp, but it's better than jail."

"Yes, I have to agree with you there."

After they were finished with the tasks the group leaders had them stand in line as the leaders counted everyone. They were to go pick up trash along the highway and then have lunch. After they ate, they loaded the bus and headed back to the camp.

At camp, they met in the Annex building and Mr. Willard made announcements. He told them to go back to the dorms and sometime later they'd be allowed to go swimming. Since several tried to escape, they were sent to the dorms and not allowed to go to the pool.

During the second week of the fourth month, the staff took turns leading the boys on a five-mile hike beyond the camp. While Johnny was hiking back to camp, he stumbled on a large rock. The pain was immediate; he knew he'd twisted his ankle. He called out to the staff leader at the front of the hikers. The staff leader knew Johnny's injury would mean no more hiking. The leader radioed for transportation and Johnny returned to camp in a Jeep.

The medical staff member looked Johnny over and stressed that Johnny needed to stay off the ankle until it healed, possibly as long as six weeks. Six weeks would mean limited activity, until the middle or so of month five.

They started the fifth month as usual with a group meeting in the Annex building to discuss the routine for the month. Director Willard insisted on a one-mile hike for the girls; the boys would go hiking later. The girls' hike was a huge success, except for a couple of girls who complained of heat exhaustion. The teens were also scheduled to do community service.

Things progressed smoothly as the month went on. The boys' hike was successful and the day was perfect. Mr. Coolridge sent Johnny over to the clinic for a check-up because six weeks has passed since his injury. The medical staff determined that

Johnny could be released and go with the others on the hike. The group leaders pointed out some friendly elk in the woods, and the teens were thrilled to see wildlife so close up.

The leaders also warned the guys to be on the lookout for black bears in the area. The leaders shared how there had been several incidents of people hiking in the woods who were attacked by bears and mountain lions. And, campers had been attacked in recent years, but none from Camp Change.

Johnny observed that it was a long hike back to camp. Everyone was exhausted. Back at the dorms, everyone showered and prepared for dinner. Tommy had kitchen duty and Johnny was assigned to do the laundry. After Smith and Goodwin finished their work details, they went back to their dorms and slept for several hours.

Johnny decided to write a letter to Pastor Brian. He stated that he was counting down the days until he could go home. In letters to his friends and family, he selected his words carefully, wanting to let everyone know that he was doing fine. He also said he was getting acquainted with his roommate, Tommy.

Johnny shared some of the fun activities they did in their rooms after they finished work. He talked of playing cards. Of course, gambling was out, so the guys just played for fun.

One evening Tommy accepted Jesus into his heart. So, Jonny asked Pastor Brian if he could keep Tommy in his prayers. Johnny added that he was ready to come home to see his family, friends, and start back to school.

After Johnny finished writing his letter, he prepared for bedtime. He prayed and asked God to help him do his best to complete the program and get to go home soon. Johnny then turned out the light and went to sleep.

The next morning, Johnny already started marking down forty more days on his calendar. He opened his Bible to start reading before the day began. He knew that God's Word would help him stay focused on completing the program.

The staff had begun putting the pressure on those juveniles who were at risk of failing the program. Johnny and Tommy were doing excellent in the program; they were determined to complete all the requirements for passing the program. It was getting close to the end of the fifth month. All the teens were anxious about who all would complete the program.

The next day, Johnny and his group were assigned to trim the trees in the park and pick up the limbs. Other groups mowed the park and trimmed the grass around the trees.

Johnny asked, "Tommy, would you like to trade jobs for a while? I'll pick up the limbs."

Tommy agreed and they took turns to give each other a break. When they were finished, they loaded back up, picked up the trash on the edge of the highway, and returned on the bus to camp.

Week three began with heavy rains. The boys remained in their dorm rooms until the rain let up. Activities included working in various places around the camp.

By the end of the week, Tommy noticed that Johnny was not feeling well, so he contacted Mr. Coolridge. Johnny was sent to the clinic to be checked out.

The doctor determined that Johnny was suffering from an upper respiratory condition. The doctor gave him some medication to take and a note to be released from his daily work duties for a few days.

After a time of rest and improvement, Johnny returned to the same daily routine, but with lighter responsibilities. He was now washing dishes after each meal. He was excited that he only had one more the month until graduation, which he was looking forward to.

The fourth week, the group leaders took the boys on a survival hike and stayed overnight. The area where the boys camped was a secured and cleared area where they had nothing to worry about other than snakes.

The group leaders taught the boys how to survive in the wild, build a shelter, read a map, use a compass, and start a fire using sticks. Every group had certain duties to perform. Johnny washed dishes and Tommy gathered firewood.

Before the overnight adventure ended, the leaders tested the teens to see what all they'd learned. Johnny had a little difficulty with reading the topographical map and using a compass, but he did okay on first aid and the other areas. Mr. Rutledge took Johnny aside and helped him to pass the map and compass tests.

Some teens ended up with poison ivy and a few had mosquito bites. Johnny only had a few mosquito bites on his legs. It was certainly a long 24 hours; but, Johnny found it to be educational overall.

The campout included eating fish, berries, and small game animals. A few of the teens caught a rabbit and a quail in a trap they set up. And, another guy, who boasted of bravery to all the others, stabbed a rattlesnake and cooked it over the fire for the others. Johnny enjoyed eating the snake the best.

At nighttime, they all heard wolves howling in the distance. The best part of the survival trip, however, Johnny thought, was to get on the bus and head back to the camp.

At the end of the fifth month, staff leaders evaluated each teen and checked his performance to determine if he would pass or fail the program. Johnny received excellent reviews as well as high scores.

The teens who received below-average reviews performed extra duties or received no special privileges. The special privileges consisted of extra free time, fishing, swimming, and use of the recreation hall to play games or watch television.

Johnny was trying his best to maintain good behavior and follow all the rules. His longings for home were intense. And, he wanted to see Pastor Brian.

CHAPTER 12: COUNTDOWN TO CAMP GRADUATION

Month six at Camp Change had now begun. The teens maintained the same routine as previous months. The first two weeks they began to prepare for graduation. The director checked out the kids' evaluation performance records.

Johnny was performing well in all aspects of camp life. He received high evaluations from the staff regarding his performance and was recommended for an award.

During his free time, he began playing chess with Tommy, and his Bible study group was thriving as more teens were showing up, if only to satiate their curiosity. Johnny now realized that almost all the guys on his floor were attending regularly.

The third week was similar to every other week; however, fewer community service activities were on the schedule. The guys remained closer to the camp.

Johnny spent much time in the auto shop and worked in the kitchen. The teens also made arts and craft projects to either take home or to donate to an auction for the camp.

Johnny found himself enjoying many afternoons drawing or designing art projects. Most craft items were to be auctioned off at the auction, an annual event to raise money for the camp.

Some of Johnny's drawings and paintings were auctioned off and brought in money for the camp. Johnny just stood back and watched how the auction was progressing. He was proud of himself for contributing to the future of the camp.

The end table that Johnny made in wood shop sold for $250. The purchaser ensured that a few camp leaders knew how pleased he was with his beautiful and well-made purchase. Overall, the auction gleaned more than $2,000 to benefit the camp.

The fourth week, the teens went to the workshop to prepare for the graduation. The staff took the group of boys and girls to the Annex building to rehearse the graduation ceremony. In addition to the rehearsal, several campers received awards.

Johnny received an award for overall good behavior and performance. Nancy also was awarded for her performance.

Each dorm floor was given a chance to receive an award, however, only one would receive the honor — awards were given to the second floor of the boy's dorm and the first floor of the girls' dorm.

Then, the director posted the names of the camp attendees who had completed the program. The ones who had not made it to graduation day were not included on the roster.

Groups that were eligible for graduation were taken on an overnight campout by the lake. The boys slept in one tent and the girls slept in another tent on the girls' side of the camp.

The staff stirred up a fire so they could roast hot dogs, make s'mores and roast marshmallows. The teens were allowed to stay up late and share stories of their camp experiences. And, the staff leaders eagerly asked the group if they had suggestions or ideas on improvements for the program.

The following day, the staff took the group into town and allowed them to purchase items to take home. Each teen was given a certain amount of money to spend for souvenirs and trinkets before returning to camp.

Johnny purchased some memorable items for his mother, brother, and sister. He bought necklaces for his mother and sister, and a t-shirt for his brother. He also purchased a t-shirt for himself. The teens were not allowed to buy knives or any other type of weapons.

The staff checked out all the items and gave the okay for each purchase. Of course, all the teens knew the rule — if anyone was caught shoplifting, he or she would go to juvenile jail and not be allowed to graduate.

An officer was assigned out front in case anyone decided to shoplift. After all, stealing had been a part of some of the teens' lives. Where they grew up or attended school, they were oftentimes challenged by their friends or gangs to steal just for the fun of it.

While Johnny was paying for his gifts, he noticed that the officers took two boys and one girl into custody for shoplifting. Nancy and Tommy, luckily, Johnny thought, were not arrested.

Everyone was then loaded onto the buses. Head count proved that all were there. They then headed back to camp.

Once in his room, Johnny wrote letters to his family and friends. He picked up his Bible to read, but, his thoughts were roaming. He was so ready to go home.

Tommy asked Johnny what he had planned once he got home.

"I'm hoping to go back to school so that I can graduate. I have thought about trying out for the school soccer team. I also heard that my family may be throwing me a surprise party."

Johnny then asked Tommy what his plans were.

"I want to get a job so that I can be busy. I've spoken with my parents and they thought it would be a good idea to move and start over. I'm hoping to get back to school once we move."

Tommy then asked Johnny if he would like to play a game of chess. Johnny agreed and they spent several hours playing chess until it was time to go to bed.

The next few days were busy as the teens primarily did their chores and attended a counseling session for the last time. Johnny stood up and faced the group. He was feeling confident and he wanted to share his thoughts about the camp.

During the session, the counselors asked the group what they would do once they returned home. After the session, the counselors handed each boy a certificate of completion.

Then the staff took the boys to the recreation hall for free time. Johnny spent most of his free time playing chess and pool. He also took the time to read his Bible.

Then the boys continued to attend classes until the last day. They worked hard before taking an end-of-camp exam. If they passed, the credits they'd earned were applied to their academic credits at their respective high schools back home.

Johnny passed the exam with a score of 93 percent. He received a certificate of completion and credit to apply at school.

The day before graduation, a small and special service was held in the workshop. There had been no previous announcement regarding the purpose of the service — but, all the teens were required to attend. Some teens were presented brass nameplates, while others were handed white crosses that contained their names.

Johnny was quite curious as to the purpose of the gifts, so he asked a staff leader the significance. He learned that the staff would inform the teens when the time was appropriate.

Commencement time arrived. The teens lined up single-file to receive their nameplates. Those who had received crosses were asked to carry them. The teens walked to the lake where the lighthouse was. There, a boat awaited them.

The teens put on life jackets and get seated in the boat. The boys got in one boat; the girls got into another. Quickly the boats sailed across the lake to a small island.

When they reached the lighthouse, Johnny noticed a sign that read, *"Graveyard of Shame."* A pathway led into the graveyard. Small white crosses were lined up alongside the pathway.

A staff leader called out the names of those teens who had crosses and asked them to step forward. These teens were instructed to walk the pathway and place their crosses in the ground near the ones already there.

The remainder of the boys walked up to the lighthouse. The staff leader opened the door and directed them to walk up the stairs, one at a time, to the top of the lighthouse. Once they reached the top, the boys gave their nameplates to the leader who awaited them. Then, this leader presented each participant with a certificate of program completion.

When it was finally Johnny's turn to walk inside the lighthouse to walk up to the top, he noticed a plaque on the wall that read, *"This is the beginning of your new journey."*

As he started up the stairs to the top, Johnny handed the leader his nameplate. The leader placed it on the wall. He then handed Johnny his certificate. He explained that the lighthouse and the steps represented both a new hope and a new beginning for Johnny's future. The leader asked Johnny to turn on the light to represent hope.

Then the leader shook Johnny's hand and asked him to descend the stairs and send up the next person. After all the teens who had completed the program had seen their names on the Wall of Honor, the group returned to the recreation building.

At the recreation building, the leaders shared with the group which teens had completed the program successfully. The leaders shared how these teens' names were now included on the Wall of Honor in the lighthouse. The camp director stood to speak.

A silence fell over the crowd, yet, the teens were eager to hear from the director. He explained that the teens who had not successfully passed the program were now eligible to repeat the program if they chose to do so.

A few teens decided that they'd try to re-enroll. They wanted to be successful and have their records cleared. The group leaders asked these teens to hand over their crosses since they were choosing to return to the next session of camp.

The teens who did not complete the program successfully, and who did not wish to repeat the program, were asked to surrender their crosses. They would now return home without their completion certificate. And, their records, even though sealed, would remain in the legal system.

All the teens who had received their certificates were allowed to make phone calls home. It was time to notify their parents to be waiting for them when the buses arrived at the juvenile center.

Johnny was very pleased with himself for completing the program because it had been very hard work. Sometimes he'd thought a lot about how great it would be to sleep in his own bed again and not worry about the lack of sleep because of the bed checks and the constant fighting that occurred in the dorm.

Johnny knew he'd probably miss some staff members who had encouraged him and listened when he needed a shoulder. He felt like a new person and looked forward to seeing everyone back home. Yet, he knew he still needed to complete the probation requirements — find a job, attend school counseling, and report to the probation officer every week for the next six months. Obviously, the greatest requirement was to stay out of trouble. Then, Johnny would stand in front of the juvenile judge to have his sentence exonerated once and for all.

The buses loaded at the Annex building. The boys boarded one bus; the girls boarded another. The teens were given specific instructions when everyone was seated. There would only be one restroom stop.

Johnny found a seat next to a window. He was exhausted and slept all the way home. He thought about Nancy and Tommy and wondered how they were doing. Since they were not allowed to have contact with the girls, Johnny never had a chance to get Nancy's phone number or social media contact information. He did, however, obtain contact information for Tommy.

It seemed like a very long bus ride back home. Johnny's mother would be meeting him at the juvenile station to pick him up. When he called home, he asked if Pastor Hanson would be there too. Sally was joyful as she shared with her son that Pastor Hanson and his family would indeed be there.

When the buses made the restroom stop, everyone got off. A few purchased snacks and drinks. Johnny went to the restroom and then purchased a snack to take with him.

The bus driver did a quick head count to see who was back on the bus. Soon, the next stop would be the juvenile center where families and friends would be waiting.

The buses arrived at the juvenile center. The driver then told the teens they could depart and reminded them to get all of their belongings. Johnny got off the bus, grabbed his bags, and ran over to hug his family. He was excited to see everyone as he presented gifts to his mother, brother, and sister.

Then he went over to greet the Hanson family. As he gave Pastor Brian a strong hug, an overwhelming and powerful emotion overtook him. Johnny experienced freedom in that moment — freedom he'd never before had.

CHAPTER 13: THE WELCOME HOME PARTY

Pastor Brian spoke with Johnny's mom about hosting a welcome home party for Johnny. Sally thought it was a very kind gesture and she offered to help. Patrick and Gloria prepared an invitation to send out on social media for the students at school. They waited a few days for responses, yet only twelve students stated they'd attend.

"If we do not hear from anyone else by Friday, I suggest we talk to the students ourselves," Patrick shared with Gloria.

Gloria agreed. "I can't believe only twelve students responded. But, your idea sounds good."

On Friday morning, they'd still not received any more responses. Gloria realized just how few friends Johnny had at school. As she walked down the hall at school, she noticed how many students tried to avoid her. She just wanted to retaliate, asking each of them why they'd chosen to avoid her just because she was Johnny's friend.

She decided to wait until Monday, during the devotion at the flagpole, to speak to other students about attending the welcome home party at the Goodwin home. Gloria had set a plan in motion. After school, Gloria went home and spoke to her father. She wanted to share the devotion Monday morning.

"Sure, Gloria. That will be fine. Let me read through your message first."

Gloria agreed and headed to her room with a strong purpose to help Johnny, and immediately started writing her devotion. She prayed and asked God to help her write down what He wanted. She wanted to make an impact when she spoke to the students. When she finished writing, she went to her dad's office and handed him the message. He read it and was very proud of his daughter. Brian made a few suggestions for her to add to or remove from her speech. She then made some changes based on her dad's suggestions and was very pleased with the final draft.

Monday morning, Gloria spoke to the students.

"Do you remember what happened seven months ago? I was frightened, just as you guys were, when Johnny brought a gun to school and threatened to kill himself and anyone else who tried to stop him. The incident reminded me that it could happen again. We must do something about bullying at school.

"Johnny could have taken the gun and started shooting people," Gloria continued, "But, instead, he willingly turned in the gun and turned his life around," Gloria paused a moment. "What do you think would have happened if he hadn't surrendered? How many lives could have been lost?"

"This is our school and we must put a stop to the violence, the name calling, and the teasing before someone else decides to bring a gun and start shooting! My brother and I have sent out many notices on social media regarding Johnny's welcome home party. Only a few of you have said you'd come.

"Let me share with you. I have read Johnny's letters that he sent to my family and me, and I have seen a huge change in him overall," Gloria went on. "Johnny mentioned that he started a Bible study group in his dorm at Camp Change. He was also active on the soccer team. He followed the rules, did his academic work, participated in group activities, and has graduated."

"Is this the type of gratitude we should show someone who tried to make things better for himself? Why are we not supportive of one of our own classmates? How would you feel if you were in Johnny's shoes," Gloria continued.

"What would Jesus do in this situation? We should allow Him to cleanse us and help us serve God. God wants to help us — this is a promise of God found in Hebrews, Chapter 9. Think about it, friends. We can overcome with strength from Jesus. He wants to help us in our daily lives. He wants to help each and every one of us, just as he is and has been helping Johnny."

"I am asking you all to consider going to Johnny's welcome home celebration," Gloria added. "In addition, let's take up a collection so we can buy Johnny a nice gift. Let's present it to him at the party." Silence fell over students. They continued listening.

After Gloria finished her message, she stepped aside and Tina Simpson began to share with the group.

"I agree with Gloria, you guys. We need to do something nice for Johnny," Tina admonished. "I'd like to see a show of hands of how many are planning on going to the party. I'm definitely going. Come on, everyone! Let's see those hands!"

Gradually a few hands slowly started to shoot up. More hands joined in. Gloria saw that the response was good; but, she saw some students shake their heads when they agreed.

"Bring your swimsuits," she added. "The Goodwins have a swimming pool in their back yard." As soon as Gloria announced that a pool was part of the event, the overall attitude of the students changed immediately. And, Gloria's message seemed to make some students realize how fortunate they were that nothing really bad had happened that day almost seven months ago.

The next day, the junior class had enough money collected to buy Johnny a nice gift. And, Gloria received confirmations from eighteen more students that they, too, would attend the party.

After school, Gloria and Patrick went shopping to find a great gift to present to Johnny at his welcome home party. They searched and searched but came up empty-handed.

Patrick looked at his sister. "Gloria, why not wait and have Mom and Dad go with us to find something together, as a family? Maybe they will have suggestions as to what Johnny may like."

Gloria agreed. "I think that's a great idea, Patrick Hanson!" She winked gleefully at her brother. "Let's also talk with Johnny's brother and sister. They may have a good idea of what he'd like."

Patrick said, "I will talk to his brother and you can talk to his sister!" At home, Patrick called Johnny's brother Billy, then Gloria spoke with his sister, Cassandra. Patrick and Gloria came up with an idea of what to get for Johnny. Brian and Susan agreed that they would fund the refreshments and a large cake. Susan and Gloria then left to go shopping.

While Gloria selected Johnny's present, Susan went to the grocery store to purchase ingredients for the cake. While Gloria was shopping, she ran into Cassandra, Johnny's sister. Gloria suggested they shop together for Johnny. They selected an MP3 player. Gloria told the salesclerk what they wanted, then asked questions about the gaming system from the Hanson's. The salesclerk answered their questions, then took the MP3 player out of the locked display case. After they made their purchase, the teens spent a few hours window shopping and looking at makeup and clothes. Cassandra saw a beautiful dress she wanted. Cassandra held it up.

"That will look great on you, Cassandra," Gloria stated with a smile. "Why don't you try on some clothes if you have time?"

Gloria shook her head. "I have time if you want to try it on. I'm waiting for my mom to get back from the grocery store." As the girls were trying on clothes, they noticed some of their friends who were also shopping. They asked the others' opinions on some of the dresses and tops. Gloria commended that the dress looked great on Cassandra and encouraged her friend to buy it.

As the two girls finished trying on clothes, Gloria asked Cassandra if she would like to come over sometime for a visit. Cassandra said she'd first check with her mom and then she'd let Gloria know. Gloria said, "Okay. Call me later and let me know what your mother said."

While Gloria was paying for the gift, Susan walked in. "Gloria I've been waiting in the car for two hours wondering what you were doing. Maybe next time you can text me?"

Gloria faced her mom and explained apologetically that she was looking at dresses with Cassandra, Johnny's sister. Gloria then spied Cassandra in the parking lot as they were leaving. Susan turned and waved at Cassandra. "Gloria, I'm happy that you and Cassandra ran into each other," she remarked. "She seems like a sweet girl."

When they got home, Gloria helped her mother with the groceries and went inside to wrap the gift for Johnny. Gloria asked Patrick if he wanted to help. "No," Patrick replied. "I need to text George Dillings to see if he can arrange for the school band to play at Johnny's welcome home party."

Gloria went upstairs and started wrapping the gift. Patrick called George, who agreed to play at Johnny's party. He told Patrick he would make the necessary arrangements with the other band members. Patrick was thrilled that the music situation was settled. George was a good friend and he always came through.

Patrick then went upstairs to ask Gloria what she bought for Johnny. She replied that she'd selected a gaming system. Later on, Gloria's cell phone rang. It was Cassandra letting Gloria know that she would be able to come over later.

"Okay. What time will you be over?"

Cassandra said she'd arrive after dinner. The two friends visited on the phone for several minutes, talking about a few of the guys at school, and the new dress that Cassandra had purchased earlier. Cassandra went to Gloria's after dinner. The girls hung out in Gloria's bedroom. Cassandra planned to wear her new dress to the party. She and Gloria began surveying Gloria's closet to find the perfect party outfit for Gloria.

The following week, the Hansons were busy getting everything ready for the welcome home party. Brian made arrangements with the church to help out with the food and drinks. Some ladies from the church called Susan to let her know they would bring over food trays. Susan planned to bake a wonderful cake. She texted Sally to see if Sally needed help with the decorations. Sally had everything under control regarding the decorations and the punch. Sally planned to set up the party in the back, next to the pool.

Brian learned from his teens that a few students decided they wanted to come to the party after all. Brian found this to be odd; he wondered just what had changed their minds. And, he was pondering how the students would treat Johnny once Johnny returned to school. But, Brian did know something for sure — he and his family were very eager to see the new Johnny and they'd be welcoming him with open arms.

Brian was amazed at how fast the months had gone by. He wondered how much Johnny had changed since he last saw him. Brian prayed Johnny had kept his faith up, because that is what Johnny wanted. Brian hoped everything was ready for the surprise party when Johnny arrived. Everyone would show up early and then remain silently in the backyard until Johnny showed up.

Susan had baked a wonderful chocolate cake. Sally made an amazing lime punch that the teens devoured. Brian estimated that about thirty students from the high school showed up. Many gifts were placed on the gift table for Johnny.

It certainly was a beautiful day to have the party. Brian wasn't sure at first if it would be a nice day since there'd been a chance of rain forecasted. If it had rained, Sally had alternative arrangements to move the party to the restaurant where she worked. However, the day turned out to be wonderful for Johnny's homecoming.

When Johnny walked into the yard, Pastor Hanson almost did not recognize him. The others had the same response too. Johnny's overall appearance had really changed. He wore a gray-striped shirt tucked into some pressed jeans. He no longer had glasses; he was wearing contacts. And, he'd just made a visit to the barber shop so that he'd have a fresh haircut.

Brian was very pleased that all the teens and adults greeted Johnny with kindness, as if there'd never been a rocky past. Johnny visited shyly at first, but, began to open up and talk with his peers as all of them stood around eating and enjoying themselves around the pool.

Johnny told everyone how sorry he was. He said he was truly surprised to have so many friends there to support him. Johnny walked over to George Dillings and thanked him for being a friend — a friend whom Johnny never knew. Johnny talked of the good times at camp, revealing how he'd played soccer and was one of the best players at Camp Change.

He shared with a few guys that he was considering trying out for the soccer team in the fall. Johnny seemed quite interested in pursuing new things.

The students continued to ask questions. They wanted to know when Johnny was returning to school, what it was like being in juvenile jail, and what the daily routine of the camp was like. They were also curious to know if Johnny had met any friends or girls. Johnny replied that he'd try to answer all their questions later, but, for now, he was ready for a large piece of Susan's cake.

Susan brought out the cake and everyone enjoyed cake and ice cream. Afterwards, Johnny opened all the presents he'd received. The first gift he opened was a new soccer ball from his mother. The next gift was an MP3 player from his classmates.

Next he opened the gift from the Hanson family. It was a PlayStation. Johnny received some new clothes from his mother and George gave him a few music CDs.

The last gift was one he'd set aside — a gold chain necklace from Tina Simson. When he finished opening the last gift, he turned to everyone and thanked them for the wonderful gifts. Johnny felt very blessed to receive such nice presents.

Johnny shared his plans to return to school when the next semester started. He also talked about his experience in prison and at the camp. He mentioned that he met some friends at the camp during his stay there. Johnny told them he saw some girls, but he wasn't allowed to communicate with them.

He explained that they were separated at all times except when they had dances. During the dance, they could not sit together; they were only allowed to dance. Johnny shared quietly with a few friends who were hanging out by the tiki lamps that he'd met Nancy Williams and that they'd danced all evening. He added that he was not even allowed to sit with Nancy at mealtime.

Johnny glanced around. He was impressed with the love he received. He remembered how he desired to share about the significance of the lighthouse. He talked of walking up the stairs to the top of the lighthouse and seeing his nameplate on the wall.

He explained how the director was at the top, waiting for the attendees so he could hand them their certificates of completion. The purpose, Johnny explained, was to honor the teens' journey of hope and a new beginning. He added that he felt sorry for those who had to walk to the graveyard of shame, and for those who decided to retake the program.

Johnny enjoyed the bonfire and seeing the lighthouse light up way into the night to signify program completion. He shared how he experienced a truly overwhelming, but happy, moment.

"The light represents our bright futures, and we can indeed move forward from our experiences." Johnny concluded, "This is all I feel like talking about right now, you guys. It was overall a very good experience. I appreciate all of you. Thanks for being here at my homecoming. It means a lot to me."

Chapter 14: Johnny's Return to School

The first meeting with Johnny's probation officer went well. The officer looked over Johnny's case and explained that everything was in good shape and going well. The officer stated in his report that Johnny soon must schedule an appointment with his school counselor once he re-enrolled in school.

Johnny stood up and shook his probation officer's hand. "Thank you, sir. I will see you in about a week and I will schedule those appointments." Johnny knew he had to watch what he did so as to be in good standing with his probation officer and the court.

Each week Johnny reported to his probation officer. He mentioned in his sessions that he was enjoying school again and had joined both the soccer and track teams. Johnny knew he'd do well as long as he stayed out of trouble.

The next several months, Johnny attended his sessions with the probation officer, although they met somewhat sporadically as Johnny missed a few of his meetings. Each time, Johnny received an excellent review on his report. However, the most recent visit did not result in a good report. The officer was direct as he listed the two big requirements that Johnny had not done — find a job and report in regularly. Johnny received a reprimand from his probation officer stating that he'd need to get a job immediately or be in violation of his probation.

As his probation officer requested, Johnny found employment at a Mexican restaurant called South of the Border. He was now a dishwasher at the same place where his mom had been a server for many years.

Johnny notified his probation officer of the job and continued reporting in until his six months ended. He was scheduled to report back to the juvenile court the following week.

The judge looked over Johnny's case file from his probation officer and granted an exoneration. Johnny's record was clear and he was released from probation. He immediately felt relieved to be off of probation and to have his record exonerated. The judge also explained to Johnny that if he got arrested for anything else it would be reinstated in his juvenile record.

The next morning, Johnny awakened early to get ready to be readmitted to school. Sally fixed breakfast for their family and was ready to go to work. She explained to Johnny that the principal wanted to see him before classes began that morning. Casandra helped set the table and get breakfast ready. Billy was showering and was already running late for school.

Sally and Casandra waited for everyone to be seated before they served breakfast. Johnny shared with his mother that he wanted to continue going to art classes and he wanted to try out for sports this semester. Sally was thrilled to see her son involved in school; yet, she was also concerned how the students would treat Johnny when he returned.

After everyone finished eating breakfast, they loaded into the car. Sally dropped off her kids at school and told them to have a great day. Then she headed into town to run errands before her work shift began.

Johnny was eager to join the other students around the flagpole. The students were extremely surprised to see how much

Johnny had changed. Johnny got up and shared his testimony. Some students asked a few questions about his time in jail.

Johnny shared his experience and then went to the office to file for re-admittance to school. As Johnny walked into the office, the principal noticed how much he'd changed. Mrs. Jackson asked Johnny if he'd completed all the requirements for re-admittance. Johnny replied that he had, except for the counseling sessions. Johnny then explained to the principal that he scheduled to meet with the school counselor after he left her office.

The principal advised Johnny that he'd be admitted as a junior and that he was now re-enrolled as a student again. Johnny made sure that his class schedule included an art class, woodshop, and some of the advanced courses he wanted so that he could prepare for college.

Johnny then looked directly at Mrs. Jackson. He felt bold and strong as he sincerely apologized to her for bringing a firearm to school and scaring the students. He knew this apologetic statement needed to be said; after all, he now believed that he was a stronger person overall.

He gathered his books for classes. He stopped at the counselor's office and scheduled appointments with Mr. Fannigan. Mr. Fannigan took one look at Johnny and was surprised to see him in his office and he was surprised at how Johnny seemed changed.

Mr. Fannigan asked if four sessions would meet the requirements of the court. Johnny replied, "Yes."

The two scheduled consecutive Wednesday morning meetings so Johnny could discuss problems, school concerns, or anything else he wanted to talk about. Mr. Fannigan suggested to Johnny to get more involved in activities and possibly to add sports to his schedule. Johnny nodded his head in agreement. He mentioned how he was considering both soccer and track. Johnny added that he wanted to ask his art teacher about entering his paintings into the state competition. Then Johnny shared about some of the things he made while at camp and how he was pleased with the projects and how they turned out.

Mr. Fannigan said that Johnny was welcome to come to his office anytime. Johnny still had concerns about the reactions he'd receive from other students who may notice Johnny going to counseling. He pondered this scenario in his mind. He felt worried, thinking that the students may see his need for counseling as an opportunity to tease him even more.

When Johnny mentioned his concerns to Mr. Fannigan, the counselor told Johnny not to worry about what people may say. Mr. Fannigan reminded Johnny that if any students said anything negative, to be sure to report it. Mr. Fannigan emphasized that he didn't want Johnny to get into trouble. Johnny finished his counseling session and headed to class. The bell rang. Mr. Fannigan handed Johnny a note to excuse him for being late.

When Johnny entered the math classroom, Mr. Blackford asked Johnny if he had a tardy note. Johnny handed him the note and Mr. Blackford asked Johnny to take a seat. Johnny went to take his seat. He was keenly aware of the whisper of the students talking about him as he sat at his desk.

Robert Carter whispered something to Greg Stevenson about seeing Johnny coming from the counselor's office. Johnny raised his hand. He asked Mr. Blackford if he could speak to the class.

Mr. Blackford agreed and told the class to listen to what Johnny had to say. Johnny stood up and walked to the front of the classroom. He began speaking and apologized to his peers about the firearm and scaring everyone that morning. Johnny mentioned to the class about the campaign posters he saw in the hallway and commented on the posters. He added that it is up to all the students to make a difference and be an example to others. Johnny also said, a bit sarcastically, that if they had no plans to take heed of the slogans on the wall posters, that it may be best to remove the posters.

Johnny shared with the students in the classroom on how much he appreciated the opportunity to return to school. He turned to Mr. Blackford and thanked him for allowing him to speak to the class. Victoria Smith waited for a while and then stood and agreed with Johnny. She shared a heartfelt message regarding how the students should take a stand against bullying.

"Good morning, class. My name is Victoria and I'm proud to call myself a Wildcat. I want to thank Mr. Blackford for allowing me to speak to you."

"I stand in front of the class and look at all your faces. I saw the same faces a year ago on the football field as we gathered in small groups. I ask myself these questions: Why is my heart broken? Why was that just a one-time event?"

"This morning I was walking down the hallways. I saw posters hanging on the wall, containing slogans about taking a stance against bullying. I also see posters that support our football, basketball, and soccer teams. Just because I am not a cheerleader or a jock doesn't mean that I don't care about my fellow classmates. Right now, however, I'm ashamed of what I see in the hallways, locker rooms, classrooms, and cafeteria. Don't get me wrong. I love my school and I'm proud to support my teams by attending the games."

"But, bigger than all of that, is what else I see. I witness name calling, teasing, and fighting. I have noticed Mr. Hanson gathering around the flagpole every morning, trying to make a difference in our school. Our goal is that no student we know would be so inclined to take his or her own life because of bullying."

"And, like you, I listened to Mr. Hanson and his family during the school assembly, sharing about the loss of their daughter. We all should remember that some of our own alumni died in years past, but, we just forget or ignore these facts."

"Every time I hear about a school assembly, I wonder who else died because of bullying. It is time that we take a stand against bullying and help end it. Maybe we can all gather on the football field or in the gym, as we did before, and start caring about each other and encouraging each other. I want more than anything to be proud of attending this school. I do not want to be afraid of walking down the hallways in my own school."

"I have watched the news and I hear about other schools that are having school shootings and students taking their own lives because of bullying,' she continued. "I don't want to see our school on the news. Let's not be the topic of another school shooting. I want to see our school make a difference and be something we all can be proud of."

"I want to see our school on the news for something good. I want to feel safe walking down the hallways. I want to see a change and be able to take a stand against bullying, school violence, and teen suicides. Who is willing to stand with me and be a positive role model for our classmates? Who is willing to show other schools that we can make a difference and that we can have a safe environment in which to achieve our education?"

Victoria reminded the students that this was their school and that they needed to be examples and stand up as leaders. Then, one by one, all of the students stood up and started applauding Johnny for what Johnny and Victoria had just boldly shared in their messages.

Mr. Blackford stood up from his desk, congratulated both students for taking a stand against bullying, and then began to applaud. He asked the class to take their seats and get ready for the dismissal bell to ring.

At the door, Mr. Blackford stopped both Johnny and Victoria and suggested they speak to the students at an assembly. Johnny waited a moment, then looked at Victoria, and the two shook their heads in agreement.

Johnny spoke with his instructors to see if he could enter his paintings and woodwork projects in a contest. Johnny's art instructor, Victoria Dorsett, wanted to see some of his work before making her decision. She was impressed with Johnny's drawings and invited him to join the high school's art league.

In class, Mrs. Dorsett asked everyone to get started on their art projects and she assigned Johnny a project. He continued to impress everyone with his painting abilities. Mrs. Dorsett roamed the classroom, observing the students' projects.

Mrs. Dorsett stopped at Johnny's painting and admired it. She noticed that his work had depth and meaning, which impressed her. She admonished him to keep up the good work and said she wanted to suggest that he consider submitting his painting at the next art fair.

After class, Mrs. Dorsett told Johnny to go online and register for the art fair. The purpose of the art fair was to raise funds to help support the art league and for students to receive college scholarships.

The art fair was quite popular in the area; several students had won various awards in past years. Some students even had sold paintings to art collectors. Johnny was boldly determined to enter his best painting. The art fair would be coming up soon.

Johnny went to his woodshop class to show his instructor, David Vangier, some of his wood projects he made at the camp. Mr. Vangier looked at the projects and was impressed.

He asked Johnny if he would be interested in entering a project into a state competition for high school students' woodshop projects. The winner would go on to the national competition. Johnny said he'd be interested. He added that he'd make another end table.

Mr. Vangier said he'd look at the end table and then decide if it would make for a good entry. Johnny knew he had only two weeks to complete the project to be eligible for state competition. Mr. Vangier also stated that he believed his students could make exceptional projects—projects that could win at the state level and advance to the national competition.

Millsville High had never before had a student advance to the national competition; but, this year was different. Mr. Vangier believed his students had a very good chance of sending at least one student to the competition.

Johnny was excited to think that he may have a chance of winning the state competition. He was determined to do his best. He worked hard to complete his end table in time for the state competition. Mr. Vangier was impressed, gave Johnny a score of 100 for the project, and highly recommended that Johnny go online soon and register.

Other students in the class were amazed by the craftsmanship and details that Johnny had incorporated into his work. They encouraged him to apply for the state-level competition.

After school, Johnny spoke with the soccer coach, the track coach, and the swim team coach. He asked them if he could try out for their teams. Both the soccer and track coaches told Johnny they would let him know after they looked over his grades. Good academic status was the first requirement for enlistment to the teams.

Johnny was looking forward to making at least one athletic team. He soon heard from the soccer and track coaches, who asked him to report to practice after school. The soccer team practiced Mondays, Tuesdays, and Thursdays from 5 p.m. to 6 p.m. The track team practiced daily from 3:30 p.m. to 4:30 p.m.

As the dedicated young man he'd become, Johnny found himself working hard at practice for six weeks. Then, the coaches posted the team members names on the board outside of the gym. Johnny looked at the board and saw his name on the list of junior varsity soccer team members.

He'd been assigned the position of right wing forward, second string. He then noticed that his name was also on the track team roster. He was already slated to run in the 5k race and the relay race.

All the guys on the team congratulated Johnny on making the team. He was excited that he'd made the teams. "Finally, all the hard work I put into the practice paid off. Now, I'm on the teams," Johnny thought to himself, with a grin on his face. He was pleased, knowing his perseverance had earned him two new athletic roles.

Johnny's mom arrived after practice let out. She was pleased that her son had made both teams. And, Johnny was quite eager to share the good news with Pastor Brian.

Johnny quickly called Pastor Brian and told him the good news. Johnny asked if he could attend the Wednesday night youth group at the Methodist Church. Of course, Pastor Brian was elated that Johnny wanted to participate. So, the two agreed to visit a bit after youth group.

After Johnny put down his phone, his mom said she had something to tell him. She shared briefly and directly that her divorce was now final. She shared with her son that she'd made the company of another man — a man named Roger Mannings, a police officer. Johnny was really shocked to hear the news of the divorce; yet, he was happy for his mom. Sally then mentioned that Roger would be coming that evening for dinner.

The next couple of days went well for Johnny. Most of the students at school treated him kindly and smiled as they passed by. Almost everyone was nice, except for a few who still perceived Johnny to be odd.

Johnny had hoped, too, that making the teams would help him become more popular with the students, but, it didn't really turn out that way. He was determined, however, not to let the opinions of a few students blur his vision of doing well this school year.

He continued to enjoy practice sessions and being a part of the teams. One afternoon, after practice, he noticed the two guys who had been picking on him and teasing him. The guys were Robert Carter and Greg Stevenson, both football players. They had a habit of sometimes shoving Johnny into a locker in the hallway and laughing about it. And, sometimes, they'd just walk by and rudely stare. But, Johnny was taking the upper road. He chose to just walk away as if nothing really bothered him.

Johnny was excited about Saturday's upcoming soccer game. He was hoping the coach would put him in. Since he was on the second string, he would have to wait until the coach chose to put him in the game. Johnny knew in his heart that he was ready to play; yet, he was still just sitting on the bench, waiting.

Suddenly, it was halftime. The score was the Wildcats 12 and the Blue Hawks 14. At the halftime break, the coach asked Johnny to get ready to play. Johnny was wearing the #17 jersey.

Johnny had the ball and dribbled it down the field. Johnny made a great pass to Patrick, #12, then Patrick passed it back to Johnny. Then Johnny shot and scored. Everyone was cheering, "Go, Johnny! Great job, Johnny!"

The Blue Hawks now had the ball. But, Johnny stole the ball and passed it again to Patrick, who passed the ball to another player, who then passed it to Johnny, but Johnny missed.

The Blue Hawks attempted at that point to kick in a goal, but Johnny blocked it and immediately scored another point. Now the game was tied, 14-14.

The Blue Hawks passed the ball, and the player dribbled it down the field. He kicked and missed the goal. The goalie kicked the ball down the field toward Johnny, who dribbled the ball and passed it to #7. Then #7 dribbled the ball and passed it off to Patrick, who passed the ball to Johnny. The ball hit the goalie's leg and went into the goal for another score.

The Blue Hawks only had one minute left in the game to score. They passed the ball, Johnny stole it, and dribbled it down the field. There he easily scored another point.

The referee blew the whistle at the second mark and the game was over. The Wildcats had won! Everyone was cheering for Johnny and congratulating him for scoring the winning goals.

Afterwards, the team asked Johnny if he'd be interested in going to a party. He replied that he couldn't make it. Then, Johnny asked what type of party it was. When Johnny learned that it was a pizza party, he quickly replied, "Sure, I'd love to go."

Johnny had initially believed that it may be a beer drinking party, and, he knew that he had to certainly avoid alcohol. But, pizza was a different story altogether. He was eager to spend time with his teammates.

They all loaded into their vehicles and drove to the pizza parlor to celebrate their victory over the Blue Hawks.

The pizza parlor was very busy when they arrived, and they notified the waitress that they needed a table for twenty people. The waitress brought their drinks over to the table, and everyone ordered the buffet.

Afterwards, they went to the skate park to skateboard. Johnny was excellent on the skateboard, just like a natural. His friends were amazed at how well Johnny took all the twists and turns in the concrete bowl. Even some said he looked as if he'd skateboarded for years.

Everyone enjoyed the recreation and had a great time. Then, after the skating had stolen their energy, the teens went home.

The weekend of the art fair had arrived. Johnny entered his painting to be judged. The day of the fair, everyone in the community came to support the school and the art exhibits.

Johnny's family and Mr. Mannings went also to show support. Now it was time for the judges to make their rounds and review all the work.

Everyone waited patiently as the judge placed a blue ribbon for 1st place on Johnny's painting. Johnny was relieved and happy that he got first place. He knew he'd worked hard and diligently for this award.

Then the state competition came around for the woodshop students. The judges closely reviewed all the woodworking entries. Johnny received a 2nd place red ribbon for his end table.

Sally was beyond excited and pleased that her son had received an award for his talent. After the judging and the announcements of the winners, everyone stood and applauded Johnny for his achievements.

Johnny returned to school Monday as usual. It seemed as if nothing had changed. Some of the guys were still picking on Johnny and whispering hostile statements under their breath. Johnny was concerned and approached Pastor Brian.

Brian reminded Johnny to be strong and closely watch his own reactions toward the students. And, Brian told Johnny to be sure to inform the principal and the school counselor.

Johnny looked at Pastor Brian. He said that he thought maybe, just maybe, if he could get some achievements and be involved in sports, things would finally be different for him. After all, deep down inside, he did want to be popular and he wanted to have friends at school.

Brian reminded Johnny as he reached over and put his hand on Johnny's shoulder, "Johnny, you can't change anything or anyone by selfish gain or by the way you look. To make a difference, Johnny, you need to be a catalyst for change."

"The type of change I'm talking about is the change of hearts that needs to happen," Brian admonished. "We need to change the hearts of those around us. You need to change the hearts of the teens at school. Just be yourself and allow Jesus to work through you to change their hearts."

Chapter 15: A Night To Remember

The seniors were excited about graduating in May. Johnny was still having difficulty getting along with some of his classmates. He was a good soccer player and was also good in track. Pastor Brian believed that Johnny had made a few friends, but, Johnny was still trying to ask Patricia out on a date. Every time Patricia turned Johnny down, all the other girls did too. Everyone thought he was okay as a friend, but some students still felt strange being around Johnny.

It was time for the junior/senior prom. The juniors decorated the gym for the seniors and the theme of the evening was "Night to Remember." The gym was decorated in blue and black with silver stars and a full moon. A porch swing with white trellises on either side had been staged for prom pictures.

The sophomores decorated the school cafeteria for the junior prom with the theme "Under the Sea." Decorations included fish and other ocean creatures. The picture booth resembled a real underwater scene.

All week, the students were setting up dates, renting tuxedos, and buying prom dresses. Gloria found a really nice, full-length satin dress. It was royal blue with sparkling silver around the neckline. She had difficulty trying to decide if she should wear her hair in an updo, so she asked her mother for help.

Susan and Gloria spent a few hours in the bathroom in front of the mirror. They wanted to make sure Gloria's hair looked perfect. They agreed that she looked dressy with an updo. And, they labored over just the right look for Gloria's makeup.

Just before she was ready to head downstairs, Gloria added a silver sash around her waist. Before she descended the stairs, her date, Tom Rawlings, had rang the doorbell. He looked quite handsome in his navy-blue tux. He was carrying a white corsage for Gloria.

Patrick came downstairs wearing a white tuxedo. He yelled upstairs to let Gloria know that her date had arrived. A few minutes later, Alysia arrived, dressed elegantly in a mid-calf length silver dress. She was wearing high-heeled, silver stilettos that perfectly matched her dress.

Gloria came downstairs while Patrick and Alysia were in the living room pinning Alysia's white corsage to her dress. Gloria and Tom joined them and Tom pinned Gloria's corsage on her. Susan quickly grabbed the camera to capture the moment. She was so proud of these teens and how nice they all looked.

Brian walked in from the kitchen. He told the teens how nice they looked. Patrick and Tom had hired a limousine to take their dates to the prom. But, first, they had to swing by Alysia's house so that her parents could take pictures. Then the group headed toward school for their prom.

The chauffeur driver dropped off the teens in front of the gym. A red carpet paved the way to the gym and cafeteria. Patrick immediately saw Johnny and noticed that Johnny didn't have a date. Johnny was discouraged. He truly had believed he'd not be alone on this important evening. He dressed up nicely in a sleek black and white tux.

Patrick and Alysia walked over to Johnny and asked if he was okay. Johnny replied that he was fine. He was not about to let it bother him that he was solo; he'd just go home if he didn't have anyone to dance and hang out with.

Patrick and Alysia suggested to Johnny that they felt he should stay and wait to see what happens. Johnny agreed he would stay longer. Patrick looked over to Alysia and asked if she wanted some punch. Alysia walked over to find a table so she could wait for Patrick to return with the drinks.

A few minutes later Patrick returned. He put the drinks on the table and extended his hand to Alysia. He wanted to make sure he got the first dance with his lovely date.

As the junior high students were on the dance floor dancing, Patrick glanced over and saw Johnny sitting at a table Johnny was hopeful that he'd find someone to dance with. While Patrick and Alysia were dancing, Patrick mentioned to Alysia she could ask one of the girls to dance with Johnny. Alysia smiled and said she would try and ask around after they finished the dance.

Alysia walked over to some of the girls who had come without dates. She kindly and softly asked if any of them would be willing to dance with Johnny. Alysia noticed that Barbara Holt did not have a date and so Alysia walked toward Barbara. Barbara glanced up and saw Alysia approaching. She already had an idea as to what was on Alysia's mind.

Barbara was reluctant at first. She asked Alysia if any other girls had agreed to dance with Johnny. Alysia replied that she'd already asked several others and they turned her down. She was hoping Barbara would say yes, but instead she got a "maybe, if no one else does." After some discussion, Barbara finally agreed to dance with Johnny, so she casually walked to Johnny's table and asked him to dance. The two ended up dancing all evening and enjoyed talking with each other.

Before the prom ended, Patrick and Tom left in the limousine and went back to their houses to get their vehicles, change clothes, and return to pick up their dates from the school.

After the cleaning crew turned off the lights in the gym and the cafeteria, everyone else headed to the bowling alley after they had changed into casual clothes. They bowled a few games, ate pizza, and socialized. Johnny walked into the bowling alley just as Barbara was arriving and joined the others already there.

While the boys were talking, the girls left and went to the restroom. Alysia asked Barbara if she liked Johnny and if she had a nice time. Barbara told Alysia that she only liked him as a friend and that, yes, she'd had a good time.

Patrick asked Johnny if he had a good time at the prom. Johnny replied that he did and they talked about soccer and track. The girls all returned to their tables and asked if everyone was ready to leave. The teens realized it was getting late, so they left and headed home.

Monday morning after the devotion, Johnny talked with Pastor Brian. He mentioned how much he appreciated Brian's help and told Brian that he considered him to be a true friend.

Johnny had become really good friends with Brian and had been attending church on a regular basis. Now his question to Brian was regarding baptism. He wanted to get baptized soon. Brian was elated and stated that it could be arranged.

The seniors were excited to play their first basketball game as seniors. Some seniors made plans for an after-game party to highlight the specialness of this game — the parents of the seniors would be honored during halftime.

The basketball team won the game Friday night as expected. The excitement in the gym was gleeful. All of the senior class was invited to come for the after-game party. Most of the seniors liked to party, and, because many of them were already 18, they sometimes brought alcohol to their parties.

Johnny didn't go to the party because he wanted to be rested for his Saturday soccer game. And, of course, he was trying to be reasonable and logical. He didn't drink, and besides, his mom's new boyfriend was a police officer.

Johnny decided to go home and watch television after the game. He didn't want to go back to jail; after all, once was enough for him. Gloria heard that Patricia, Christina, Alan, Tina, Carl, and Fred planned to attend the party.

Tina called Gloria from the party around 10 p.m. Tina stated she was worried about Alan because he'd been drinking. Christina, too, was afraid something might happen. She also heard Patricia and Alan arguing over the car keys. Tina stressed to Gloria that her brother wasn't drinking.

Gloria finished talking to Tina. She knocked on her father's bedroom door. She explained to her dad what she'd just learned from the students who were at the party. Alan was drinking too much and was very drunk. Brian knew that Patricia and Christina didn't drink because they knew better. All the teens, however, were there for the overall atmosphere, which consisted of pizza, beer, and music.

Gloria heard from Tina that the party lasted until midnight. Brian wondered why no parents were attending and whose house it was. Gloria replied that she knew that they had all congregated at Fred Carlson's house because his parents were out of town for the weekend. Fred didn't know that someone had brought beer inside, apparently through the back door.

Tina told Gloria that she was afraid the police would show up and arrest everyone at the party, so she had left early, somewhere around 11 p.m.

Brian got on the phone and spoke with Carl. He knew Carl well enough to believe that Carl would tell him the truth. Brian asked Carl what had happened after Tina left.

Carl replied, "The party was getting out of hand, and several students were drunk and staggering outside." Some students stood out in the yard; others were inside dancing. Carl said he'd noticed that a few students went upstairs. Others, he added, were hanging out in the kitchen, eating.

Carl was really nervous because the police usually patrolled the neighborhood. He'd asked the students who were outside to come in. Finally, they all did. Carl got out a card table and encouraged a few of the students to play cards. He believed he remembered seeing Patricia and Christina sitting at the card table.

Carl recalled that he thought some students were upstairs behind closed doors, possibly misbehaving. He had noticed too that some teens were asleep downstairs on the sofa and the floor. Carl heard Alan talking to Patricia about going somewhere after the party. He didn't know what they were discussing, except what he heard about going somewhere to make out. Carl thought he heard Patricia arguing with Alan, and heard her say, "No, I just want to play some more cards."

"Patricia told Alan she wanted to play some more cards before she left to go home," Carl continued. "She asked Alan to join them and to relax. Alan finally joined the card game, even though he really wanted to head out with Patricia. I also overheard Patricia talking to Christina, who was trying to get Patricia and Alan to stay there for the night and sleep it off."

"Christina turned around and went back to playing cards with Fred and me," he said. "It was getting close to midnight. The card game got pretty interesting, and then everyone got tired of playing cards."

Brian then asked Carl what time Patricia and Alan left the party. It was probably around midnight; best Carl could recall.

Carl continued talking to Pastor Brian. He knew that Christina was still trying to convince Patricia and Alan to stay at the house. Carl heard Christina say, "Patricia, Alan is not fit to drive you home." Patricia reassured Christina she would be fine. Carl, likewise, tried to convince Alan to let him drive the two of them home.

Then, when Carl noticed Alan still had his keys in his hands, Carl knew Alan was planning to drive no matter what. Christina and Carl had tried to stop them, but by the time they opened the door and looked out, the two had already left. Alan was behind the wheel.

Carl continued talking to the pastor on the phone. He knew that Alan drove a red 1979 Camaro that he'd received as a birthday present from his dad. Carl said he'd expressed his concerns also to Fred, informing him that Alan was driving drunk, and that he was worried that something may happen.

Pastor Brian thanked Carl and hung up. He hurriedly dressed and headed toward Fred's house, hoping he could convince some of the teens to allow him to drive them home.

As soon as he arrived, most of the teens had already left the party. Brian walked up to Fred's front door and asked if he could speak to him about the party. Fred told Brian everything he knew about what had happened at the party.

He revealed that a few students were still hanging around and they decided to crash on the sofa or on the floor. Brian asked where his parents were and learned that they'd be returning Monday from a trip. Brian didn't believe it was a good idea for the kids to remain in the house without supervision.

Brian awakened the students, told them to get up, and asked them to load into his van. He was determined to drive them home. He was still concerned about the alcohol that the teens had consumed and he wanted to know where it came from.

Fred told Brian that Alan had contacted some of his older friends who had brought the beer in through the back door. Fred didn't know these older teens, but, he had tried to learn who they were from Alan. Alan replied that they were some college friends of his and he wasn't going to say who they were.

Brian dropped off the last student at his home. It was time to head home. He was deep in thought about the teens' behavior when he heard police and ambulance sirens near him.

He'd worried greatly, hoping that Patricia and Alan had made it home safely. But, the ongoing sound of the sirens made him believe that a bad accident had occurred close by.

Around 1 a.m., Brian pulled into his driveway and went inside. Susan and the kids were still up, sitting in the living room. Gloria had still not heard if Patricia had made it home safely and she was worried. Brian shared reluctantly with his family that he suspected a bad accident, based on the number of emergency sirens he'd just heard. He began to get overly concerned about the teens who'd congregated earlier at the party. He asked Gloria, "Has anyone called for me?"

"No one has called since you left the house, dad," Gloria responded, knowing her dad was quite worried.

"All right," Brian said. "Let's all try to get some rest after we pray for those involved in the accident. I just can't shake the sounds of those sirens."

The Hansons all stood and gathered in a circle, holding hands. They began to pray.

CHAPTER 16: AN ACCIDENT IN THE NIGHT

On a dark and rainy night, a frightening call came into dispatch at approximately 1 a.m. All available police officers were to report immediately to an accident scene. The eerie sound of squad car sirens pierced the night. Officers Roger Mannings and Pete Finagan were the first to arrive at the scene.

As they approached the scene, Officer Mannings notified dispatch to send an ambulance and fire personnel. These vehicles seemed to arrive almost immediately, amidst the loud sirens as they approached the scene.

The officers immediately noticed a red 1979 Camaro turned over in a ditch and skid marks on the highway. The officers set out flairs and began to direct traffic. The emergency personnel from the ambulance and fire truck began assisting the victims. Officer Mannings notified dispatch that two teens, one male and one female, were involved in the accident and that he did not yet have any identification.

The officers directed the ambulance personnel and fire department EMTs who rushed into the ditch with stretchers. They feverishly began working on the victims and notified dispatch to send a helicopter for immediate transport. Both victims were in bad shape, they reported.

An EMT approached Officer Mannings and told him they smelled alcohol on the male victim. Officer Mannings then notified Detective Vincent, who was measuring the skid marks on the highway above the ditch and preparing a traffic investigation report. The detective instructed Officer Mannings to determine the identification of the teen behind the wheel. Both victims, they determined, were unconscious at the time of the accident.

Officer Finagan accompanied Officer Mannings to the hospital in hopes to get some answers and do a complete accident report. Officer Mannings spoke with the nurses and requested to speak to a doctor. The nurse said both victims had just gone into surgery. The nurse gave the victims' names to the officers.

Officer Mannings asked Officer Finagan to wait. Now was the most difficult part of his job. It was time to notify the teens' parents. Officer Mannings met with Detective Vincent and they left together to notify the parents.

The first stop was the Miller House. It was approximately 1:25 a.m.. The two waited in the squad card to notify dispatch that they would be out of the car for a few minutes. Dispatch called over the radio and cleared them. As they approached the house, they noticed a light was on. They knocked firmly on the front door.

Sue Anne Miller, and her husband, Clifford, were asleep. Sue Anne woke up because she heard a noise. She turned the bedroom light on to glance at the clock and listen again for the noise. She was worried about Patricia, who was not yet home. Sue Anne asked her husband if he should get up and check. Clifford calmly asked his wife not to worry. He just knew Patricia would be home soon. Sue tried to go back to sleep. Officer Mannings had waited long enough, so he rang the doorbell. Detective Vincent told Officer Mannings to wait because they knew someone was home. Sue Anne thought she heard the doorbell ring and she woke up her husband.

Clifford waited and then, he too, heard the doorbell. He glanced at the clock and looked at his wife and commented that he had no clue who'd be at their front door this late. He pulled on his pants and Sue Anne put on her robe. She and Clifford then cautiously went to the door. Clifford asked who was at the door.

"This is Detective John Vincent and Officer Roger Mannings with the police. Can we come in and talk to you?"

Detective Vincent added, "Are you Clifford Miller and do you have a daughter named Patricia?"

Clifford opened the door and greeted the officers. "Yes, please come in."

The officers in unison removed their hats as they walked into the living room. Clifford shook his head. "What did Patricia do this time? Is she at the police station?"

Detective Vincent spoke softly. "No sir. Would you and your wife please sit down so that we can talk"

Sue Anne sat on the couch next to her husband. Detective Vincent was calm. "Yes. This is about your daughter and, no, she is not in trouble."

Sue Anne turned and looked at her husband and then looked at the officers. Then she stood and began frantically yelling, screaming, and hitting her husband. "No! No! It can't be true, Oh, God! Please, not my daughter. She can't be dead!"

Detective Vincent asked Sue Anne to be calm and sit back down. He explained that Patricia was alive and in surgery. The detective then turned to his partner and motioned to Officer Mannings to explain what had happened.

"There was an accident involving a young man and your daughter. She's in the hospital. We need you to go now."

Sue Anne and Clifford jumped up off the couch. They promised the officers that they'd dress quickly and head to the hospital. The officers left the Millers' house to head to the Johanstons'. The officers got a call confirming from the scene that Alan was driving. He'd been drinking and was traveling at a high rate of speed. The investigation officer at the scene believed the driver was speeding and drunk at the time of the accident.

The officers stopped and rang the doorbell. Mr. Robert Johanston come to the door. Mr Johanston and his wife, Denise, stood at the door and she knew something was wrong. The officers shared about the accident, stating that they needed to go soon to the hospital because their son was in critical condition. Denise yelled and screamed hysterically at the officers and asked them to please tell the truth about what had happened. Detective Vincent asked Mr. Johanston if his son ever drank before.

"No, Sir. Not that we are aware." The detective said their son appeared intoxicated and that the vehicle ran off the road, resulting in an accident. Denise asked if Alan was alive and how bad he was injured. The officers said it was serious and to meet at the hospital. When the Millers arrived at the hospital, Sue Anne called Susan to see if they could come to the hospital. Clifford agreed. He headed to the nurses' station to check for updates. The nurse informed him that their daughter was in surgery. The doctor would notify them as soon as she was out.

While Clifford filled out the paperwork, Mr. Johanston arrived with his wife and they began asking questions and filling out their paperwork. Mr. Johanston asked the Millers if they'd heard anything from the doctors. Mr. Miller informed him that they had just arrived. There was nothing new to report. The two couples went together into the waiting room to wait and hope.

Near 1:45 a.m., Susan and Brian received a phone call. Susan answered and told her husband that there had been a bad accident. Brian asked who was calling. Susan replied that it was Sue Anne Miller. The Hansons dressed quickly and awakened their children. They shared that Patricia had been in an accident. They quickly loaded in the van and headed to the hospital. When they arrived, the Millers were in the waiting room. Brian asked Clifford if he knew what happened.

"I only know Alan was driving and lost control of the car, and it overturned, according to the officer who came to our house. He also mentioned that Patricia was in surgery, and I haven't heard from the doctor yet."

Susan talked with Sue Anne as both women cried. Sue Anne knew something bad had happened when the doorbell rang. She shared with Susan, "Clifford answered the door, and told me to dress and come downstairs."

Brian then heard Sue Anne tell Susan that she was going to call Christina's mother to let Christina know about the accident. Susan and Brian were waiting in the waiting room with Clifford. Brain asked his teens to go and find drinks for everyone. It was quite a long and difficult wait. They didn't know how long Patricia would be in surgery nor the extent of her injuries. The Johanstons approached from the cafeteria. Brian walked over to Robert to find out if he knew anything else. Robert knew Alan was driving. He'd been drinking and was in surgery.

The children came back with coffee and bottled water. An hour later, a doctor came out. Brian heard Denise scream hysterically as Robert was holding her. They both were crying. Brian went over to Robert, extended his hand, and asked if they needed anything. Robert said the doctor relayed that Alan died in surgery. He'd suffered from internal bleeding caused from a ruptured spleen, lacerated liver, severed aorta, and other injuries. The doctor revealed that Alan was heavily intoxicated.

Brian tried to reassure Robert. "If there's anything else you need, be sure to let us know. We love you guys and we are praying for you." Robert thanked Brian, as Brian walked over to visit with the Millers. Brian feared the worst.

The doctor said, "Patricia is still in surgery. She is doing fine, except that we're not sure if she is going to walk again." The doctors outlined Patricia's injuries — severe head injuries, minor lacerations, and a severed spinal cord.

Brian gestured to his wife and kids that he wanted to head to the chapel. The Millers joined the Hansons for prayer. They lingered a few minutes in the quietness of the chapel, observing the calming colors of the stained glass windows. The silence seemed to overcome them like a mighty wave. They all sat still and reverently, as if to be listening to the voice of God. When they returned to the waiting room, they saw Christina and her mother. Christina joined Susan, Brian, and the Millers. She asked if they knew anything else about Patricia. Brian told Christina that Alan hadn't made it; Patricia was still in surgery.

The doctor came out to speak with the Millers. His words were solemn as he stated that Patricia was out of surgery and in recovery. They believed she may never walk again. Mr. Johanston approached the Millers and offered his condolences. He said he was very sorry for what had happened in the wee hours of the morning. The police came into the waiting room just then to share the details of the accident report.

Alan Johanston, age 17, was behind the wheel of a red 1979 Camaro, intoxicated while driving. He was driving at an excessive speed when he lost control of the vehicle. The vehicle flipped several times before landing in the ditch upside down. The driver was ejected out of the windshield, and the female passenger, Patricia Miller, age 16, who was not intoxicated, was ejected out of the passenger door and was pinned under the vehicle. The accident occurred at or near 1:09 a.m. Neither the driver nor the passenger was wearing a safety device at the time of the accident."

The officers handed a copy of the incident report to both the Millers and the Johanstons. Brian told the Millers that he'd check on Patricia the next morning to see how she was doing.

"My family and I will be praying for you and Patricia. Will you please let us know if there is any kind of change with her, and if there is anything we can do for you and Sue Anne?"

"We will let you know tomorrow. Thank you for being here with us, Pastor Brian."

Brian then gestured for his family to exit the hospital. The intense darkness penetrated the night. A heavy gloom filled the air. Brian knew he'd need a strong dose of grace from God to minister to his students this week, both at the flagpole and at youth group. He knew God's Spirit would go before him.

Chapter 17: Reflection and Recovery

The next morning, the teens arrived at school and went immediately to the flagpole to pray for Patricia. Pastor Brian spoke to the crowd, stating that today's focus was to pray for their friend's healing and recovery. And, they would be praying for peace and comfort for Alan's family.

Brian asked Christina to please step up to the front and share the events that had occurred. He also wanted her account to dispel any rumors that could be floating around regarding the teens and their behavior before the accident.

Brian scanned the crowd. He immediately noticed that Johnny was seemingly taking the news very hard.

Mrs. Jackson announced over the loudspeakers that all the students report to the gym for first period.

When the students entered the gym, there was a brief moment of silence. Then, Principal Jackson walked up to the podium. She announced briefly that Alan Johanston was killed in an automobile accident and that Patricia Miller was in the hospital with serious injuries.

She then asked everyone to join her for a moment of silence. Johnny bowed his head and prayed. He petitioned God for his classmates, asking that God show them His unconditional love through this tragedy.

Mrs. Jackson then announced that a candlelight vigil was scheduled for Friday night at the Methodist Church. She then turned and thanked Pastor Brian for arranging the vigil to be held at his church. He nodded to her in agreement.

After the gathering in the gym, Brian drove in silence to the hospital to check on Patricia's status. He walked into her room and Clifford motioned for the two of them to meet in the hallway outside of her room.

"She is still unconscious, Pastor. She will be here for a long time, we believe. It's possible that she could be here at least three months, maybe longer. We just never can tell when she will wake up. All we can do for her is to be with her, and to let her know we are here."

Brian shared with Clifford that his family, his church, and the students at the high school were praying for Patricia and their family. Clifford said Patricia did not know yet that Alan had died.

He expressed to Brian that he was worried about how she would deal with the news when she did wake up. Brian shared with Clifford that he'd try to be there when she awakened so he could help with sharing the news.

Brian looked at his watch and knew he needed to head to his office. As he turned to leave, he ran into Johnny. Johnny said he left after school to come and see Patricia.

Brian shared the grim news that Patricia was still unconscious and unable to recognize her guests. Johnny replied that he understood; yet, he still wanted to speak with Clifford.

Brian went home. It was time to settle into his office and prepare his message for Wednesday night. He shared his message to an unusually quiet crowd and reminded them that the vigil would be held Friday night. And, Brian said he'd met with the band director who had plans for the band to play for the vigil.

As the start time approached, Brian had everything arranged in the church parking lot for the vigil. Brian and Pastor Cunningham began the service with prayer, asking God to make His presence known and to cover the crowd with His peace.

Brian began his message. After he spoke of the promises of Heaven and shared scripture regarding eternal life and God's love, Brian turned over the service to the football coach. The coach tried to hold back tears as he spoke of Alan's achievements, his passion for football, and his leadership as the team captain.

After the coach shared his message, he lifted up Alan's uniform jersey for the crowd to see. He made a statement of dedication, both to honor Alan and to retire Alan's number. He announced that the jersey would be displayed in the trophy case

Then Brian asked Alysia Sanders to come up and share a memorial poem and a message. Everyone knew that Alysia had a real talent for writing poems. She felt honored to share from the podium as the crowd listened intently.

The remaining speakers were Alan's parents and then the principal. Then, the crowd lit their candles and raised them above their heads in unity. The band began to play softly as everyone reflected on the purpose of the vigil and remembered their fondness for Alan.

Saturday afternoon, Pastor Hanson performed Alan's funeral. He had asked Christina if she wanted to read a poem in memory of Alan — a poem that would speak hope into the hearts of the students, as well as others attending the service.

Christina loved poetry just as Alysia did, and had written several poems. This time, however, she chose a poem by a woman in Texas, Melanie A. Martin. The poem was titled, "*How Great a Canyon.*"

Christina began:

"When distance spans time between you and me,

How great a canyon is all my eyes see.

A chasm so great and grand and rich,

Too wide to traverse and too long to bridge.

Such a marked interruption in time it is,
Truly uninvited and laden with tears.
A gulf of emotion floods over me,
Uncontrollable sadness, yet only temporarily.

And, so it is with horrendous grief—
A ravine between earth and God's eternity.
For separation is painful and full of unrest,
But, God's promise is eternity, together and blessed.
How I long for eternity where no longer will be
such a deep cleft existing between you and me.
Please wait for me and save my place —
For I know my God's plan is Amazing Grace!"

(Copyright 2019)

The crowd was silent. Many people were wiping tears from their eyes. Many were looking down in reflection. It seemed that the words of the poem resonated loud and clear —describing a real and physical canyon, not just a canyon of emotional sadness and separation.

Brian ended the service with prayer, reminding the attendees that God is the author of heaven and heaven is indeed a real place — a final resting place for those persons who have trusted God. He then reminded the crowd that eternal life with God is a promise from the Bible.

After the funeral, several students lingered to go with the family to the gravesite. At the cemetery, Brian noticed many students with tears in their eyes as they placed flowers on the casket. Some gently touched the casket and lingered; others walked by in solemnness.

As everyone turned to head to their cars, Brian and Alan's parents embraced. At that moment, a lone bluebird landed gracefully in the middle of the casket flowers. It was as if God Himself was also in their midst.

The next several weeks, the students continued to pray for Patricia's healing. Students took turns visiting her as the hospital and rehabilitation staff allowed. Brian organized special groups to continue to pray for Alan's family as well as Patricia's healing.

During one session, Patricia's parents prayed the prayer of salvation and accepted Jesus into their hearts and lives. Brian was thrilled to see that they trusted God even in the midst of their uncertainties and pain. During each prayer session or small group meeting, Sue Anne was always there to provide an update on her daughter and to encourage the teens to continue to pray.

Three months later in July, as the doctors had predicted, Patricia awakened slowly from unconsciousness. Clifford immediately called Brian and asked him to come soon to the hospital. He explained that Patricia was beginning to wake up.

When Brian arrived, Johnny was there also. Brian asked Johnny quietly to please remain in the waiting room. Clifford, Sue Anne, and Brian first needed to talk with Patricia.

At the moment Patricia became fully alert, she was surrounded by her youth pastor and her parents. The doctor came in and leaned gently over Patricia's bed. He reached down to touch her hand. His smile spoke the words that no one could voice. Everyone was gleaming with joy through their tears. Patricia scanned the room with her eyes and looked at the adults surrounding her bedside.

The doctor asked Patricia if she remembered anything about an accident. She replied that she did recall going to the after-party and leaving with Alan. After those comments, she remembered no other events, she said.

The doctor shared with her that she'd been in the hospital for twelve weeks. Now, her job was to rest and get well. The doctor then allowed Patricia's parents to share with her that she'd been in a car accident and that she'd just awakened from unconsciousness. Sue Anne shared how the doctors were very concerned at this time that Patricia may never walk again. Her injuries were big, yet only time would tell the healing outcome.

Patricia paused and silence fell over her room. The only sounds were from the machines that were monitoring Patricia's vitals. Everyone waited as she tried to process her mother's news.

Patricia looked at the adults and asked how Alan was. Sue Anne spoke softly to her daughter, watching Patricia's expressions as she explained that Alan had died shortly after they'd arrived in emergency.

"No! No! No!" Patricia screamed and yelled hysterically at her mother and tried to gesture wildly. Sue Anne asked Patricia to try to remain calm as she explained the details of the horrible night. Patricia was fighting with her bedding and the tubes in her arms and hands. She was desperate to get out of bed to go and find Alan, but it was impossible since she had no feeling in her lower body. Her dad and Pastor Brian tried to restrain her. She suddenly slipped from their grasp and fell to the floor. Her mom ran to the hallway to yell for help. Clifford pushed the call button as he was trying diligently to pick up his daughter.

On the floor, Patricia fell into a heap of emotional distress. The news of Alan's death was just too much for her. She and her dad were together in the floor, arm in arm. They just cried together. Pastor Brian knelt beside them feeling helpless. He was praying silently, asking God to bring peace to the situation.

Clifford, a nurse, and an orderly gently picked up Patricia and placed her back in bed. She was defiant and angry and suddenly began to rip out her arm and hand tubes and catheters that led to her IV and numerous machines.

Sue Anne looked on with horror as Patricia screamed as loudly and violently, saying repeatedly that she did not want to live. Sue Anne pressed the call button to get help from the nurses station. Brian and Clifford tried to hold Patricia down. In just a few minutes, two nurses came in and secured restraints to Patricia's arms. Then, a nurse gave her a sedative for sleep.

After Patricia dosed off, Brian left and went to the waiting room. He shared with Johnny that Patricia was now resting and it would be best for Johnny to return later.

Johnny said he would stay and wait until Patricia was able to see visitors. Pastor Hanson admired Johnny for his care and compassion for Patricia. The youth pastor was about to leave when he saw Christina walking in. She asked Pastor Hanson if Patricia were awake. Brian stated that Patricia was asleep, and still not yet able to have visitors. He shared with Christina that Patricia was aware of the accident and Alan's passing, but, that the nurse had given her a sedative to help her rest.

The next morning, Brian drove to the hospital to visit Patricia. She was still in restraints, yet, she was awake. She yelled for the nurse, demanding that the restraints be removed. The nurse called for help because Patricia was getting angry and attempting to get out of bed.

The nurse kindly asked Brian to leave. She stated that Patricia was not yet ready for visitors. As Brian left the room, Patricia continued to scream and yell for a doctor.

Patricia yelled, "Why don't you let me die! I hate you! I don't want to live like a cripple!"

Several more days passed before anyone was able to visit Patricia. Then next week came and Pastor Hanson walked to the nurses station. He inquired about Patricia, wondering if she were allowed visitors or if there were specific visiting hours. The nurses asked him to make his visit short and not to speak loudly with Patricia.

Patricia was moved to the rehab facility so she could begin physical therapy. Brian and his family were the first to visit her. Brian knocked on the door and asked Patricia if they could come in. He waited for her response, leaning into her room a bit to make sure he could hear her answer. She invited them in.

Brian quickly noticed that she'd received several flower arrangements containing yellow carnations and red roses. She also had a row of get-well cards hanging on the wall. Gloria and Susan brought white day lilies that made a nice contrast to the existing arrangements. Patrick handed Patricia a card from the family.

Patricia said, "Pastor Brian, please stay until my physical therapist shows up." Patricia was still weak. Brian opened his small New Testament. He shared scriptures with her and reminded her that it was important to keep her faith strong. Patricia nodded in agreement. She wanted to exhibit a strong faith, even though she was sad that her body was weak.

The therapist walked in and told Patricia that it was time to get into the wheelchair and head to therapy down the hall. Pastor Brian reassured Patricia that he'd return soon to check on her. He held his little New Testament tightly, visually reminding Patricia to hold tight to her faith in God.

Brian was leaving as Clifford and Sue Anne walked into their daughter's room. They saw that Patricia was getting ready to head to therapy. As Patricia was wheeled away, Brian lingered a moment to ask her parents her status. Mostly, he wanted to know about how long she had left in the hospital.

It was late August and school was starting. Patricia's parents shared with Brian that the doctors were saying about two more months. And, they were not sure if she'd be able to return to school at that time.

The first goal was to strengthen her upper body. Plus, she would need the cast removed from her right arm before she could be taught how to maneuver her wheelchair all by herself.

In October, about six months after the accident, Patricia was still showing signs of improvement. The cast was now off of her arm, which had healed well. She was able to sit up by herself; yet, she still could not maneuver herself into a wheelchair.

Brian shared one afternoon with Patricia that he believed she was one remarkable young lady. He was proud of her for showing perseverance and endurance. And, he talked of the Apostle Paul and how he, too, had to endure many hardships in his life.

Brian had hesitated to this point about asking who all had visited from school.

"Patricia, have you had visitors from school? Any of your classmates come to see you regularly?"

"Only two, pastor. Christina and Johnny." She thought some of her other friends would have already visited her too, but they hadn't.

"I'm a very popular girl in my classes and head cheerleader. I thought for sure some of my friends would show up," Patricia added, with sadness in her voice.

Brian tried to comfort her. He told her that maybe they just wanted her to recover and get better. She bowed her head sadly, nodding, then admitted being tired. She just wanted to rest.

Brian said he'd check on her later, so he walked out and closed the door behind him. Just then, he heard a crash in her room and turned to open the door. He and a nurse went running in together to see Patricia's lunch tray on the floor.

Patricia began screaming about why her friends had not come to see her. She began crying too, as the emotions flooded her room.

Brian quickly surmised that Patricia was probably suffering from depression. The nurses quickly secured the arm restraints to assure that Patricia would not try to hurt herself.

Brian saw that both Christina and Johnny were in the waiting room. He explained to them that Patricia was having an emotional moment. He shared how they were the only friends from school had even bothered to come and see her.

Christina asked if she and Brian could step aside so that she could talk with him. She wasn't yet willing to include Johnny on what she wanted to share with her youth pastor.

She mentioned to Brian that Patricia wasn't very nice to her friends at school, and that she, Christina, was really the only one who was actually a close friend to Patricia. Brian asked Christina about Johnny too, wondering if Johnny had come daily to the rehab center. Christina said yes and that Johnny was one remarkable and caring guy.

Brian had a change of thought. He said to Christina, "Wait a minute. Let's check at the nurses' station to see if it's okay to visit. And, let's see if Johnny wants to go with us."

Christina walked to the nurses' station and asked if they could visit Patricia. The charge nurse said they could go into her room in a few minutes, and the attending nurse would let them know when it was okay.

After a few minutes, they were invited in to visit with Patricia. They enjoyed a good time of fellowship. They could see that Patricia was quite eager to complete her physical therapy plan so she could go home as soon as possible.

The next couple of months seemed to pass slowly. Brian, however, saw some improvement in Patricia's mobility. Now she was almost able to get into the wheelchair by herself, with little assistance. Sometimes a nurse helped her; other times, she was able to hoist herself into the wheelchair.

Patricia asked Pastor Brian to push her outside for some fresh air. The two took off for the courtyard to enjoy the sunshine and the breeze.

At a table in the middle of the courtyard, Patricia revealed to her youth pastor how she'd thought of taking her own life a few times, but, that she'd never really tried. Brian realized that she was talking about suicide ideation, but that she probably never had a true plan.

Suicidal ideation is having thoughts of suicide or feeling unwanted to the point of wanting to die. Many teens suffer from suicidal ideation at times; however, it does not mean that they truly have a plan to take their own lives.

Patricia began crying. Brian leaned forward slightly to reach for her hand.

"It will be okay, Patricia. Remember, you have Jesus to give you strength and you have people who care about you." The pastor gave her hand a squeeze and leaned over to kiss her forehead. He told her, "Look," he added. "It's such a beautiful day to be outside."

After a few moments of silence, Patricia looked at Brian seriously. "Pastor Brian," she stated, "I need some help. I am ready to go to counseling."

Brian was thrilled deep down inside regarding her decision. He knew that Christian counseling could be very beneficial to helping her make progress, both emotionally and physically. After all, she had lost Alan suddenly and they never had a chance to say good-bye.

"Yes, I agree," he replied. "I'm proud of you for making this decision."

Brian told Patricia that he needed to get home. She really didn't want him to leave. He sensed the sadness in her voice, yet, he remained positive as he shared that he was quite proud of her for working to regain her physical strength.

He pushed her back to her room. Both enjoyed some small talk as they entered her room and then Brian reminded Patricia that he'd be back soon. And, he told her it would not be long before she could go home.

Brian sat in his car and had a thought. He would see if Susan and his kids would like to host a welcome home party for Patricia. He quickly texted Clifford to see what his thoughts were.

Both Sue Anne and Clifford felt honored. They agreed that such an event would be great. It would also be a good way to help lift Patricia's spirits.

The next month, Patricia was ready to leave rehab. She'd accomplished all of her goals in her daily therapy sessions. The doctors were pleased with her progress.

The Hansons eagerly prepared for the welcome home party Saturday. Susan had baked one of her popular cakes. Brian invited Christina and Johnny as well as others. However, only a few agreed to come. Tina, Samantha, Alysia, and, of course, Brian's teens, rounded out the group of teens to seven. With Patricia, the count was at eight.

The doorbell rang. Susan exclaimed excitedly, "They're here!"

Patricia looked radiant. She wore a smile on her face and her eyes sparkled. Her mom had bought her a new yellow dress. She was so very happy to be done with rehab, at least for now. She was beginning to look forward to her senior year and hanging out with her friends.

Susan instructed everyone to head to the backyard for the party. As they settled around the picnic table and the large spread of food, everyone shared just how very happy they were to have Patricia with them in this time of celebration. The teens talked joyfully about graduation day and their plans for the summer after high school.

Brian stood aside, taking in the joy of the fellowship. He silently thanked God for this moment. He realized that Patricia was touched by the generosity of cards and gifts. And, he witnessed, for the first time in a long time, genuine emotion on her face and tears in her eyes.

Patricia didn't want the well-wishers to see her tears. She smiled boldly and said she was indeed ready to return to school the next Monday.

CHAPTER 18: GOD'S GIFT — A NEW FRIEND

Monday morning, Patricia's parents took her to school. She was eager to start back to school, yet she wondered what the other students would think of her being confined to a wheelchair. Today would be her last day to use a hand-driven wheelchair; her electric one was due to be delivered that afternoon.

"How will my classmates treat me, Dad? Will they start teasing me for being disabled?"

Clifford glanced at his daughter and gently explained that she should not worry about what others may think or say. "You are still the same person on the inside," he reminded her.

After her parents dropped her off at school, Clifford went to pick up their new customized van—a van that would accommodate Patricia's electric wheelchair.

When Patricia arrived at the front entrance, to her surprise, everyone welcomed her with kindness. Christina casually strolled over to Patricia and mentioned with a grin that she and Johnny were dating. Patricia was happy for Christina. And, she asked her if she'd push her around at school that day.

"When did you guys decide to start dating?" Patricia asked.

"Well, Patricia, it was when I observed Johnny coming to visit you in the hospital every chance he had. That showed me his truly compassionate heart."

Johnny approached the girls, with a grin on his face. He stepped up beside Christina and touched her arm. Patricia smiled up at him. "You are truly a good friend," she said with a smile. Johnny was certainly a friend she did not know she had until her accident.

"I'll remember what all you and Christina did for me while I was recuperating," she said, trying to choke back her emotions.

The first bell rang. It was time for the students to head to class. Christina asked Patricia if she needed someone to go with her to her first period class. Patricia politely spoke to Christina in a soft voice, "Thank you. I appreciate the help because I need to go first to the front office."

Patricia needed to re-enroll in her classes. A few students walked by and asked if they could walk alongside her and help carry her books and lunch bag. Patricia was beginning to realize the importance of friendship and how valuable friends can be in a time of need. She willingly agreed to let them assist her.

Patricia stopped at the door of the front office and spoke to the students who had gathered around her. She was intentional in her words to her friends. She was sure to engage them in eye contact before beginning her apology.

"You guys, I need to apologize," she paused a bit, as if to gather her thoughts. "As a Christian, I have no excuse to mistreat my friends, no matter who they are. Friendship is very important," she paused again and swallowed hard. This was tough for Patricia, but, she knew she needed to continue.

"I would appreciate it if you guys would be my friends. I need you. We need each other," she added. All the students casually looked at each other, grinned, and agreed that they truly liked Patricia's proposition.

Patricia began crying, tears rolling down her cheek. "I'll never be a cheerleader again." There was silence for a few moments. The other cheerleaders were filled with emotion for their friend.

They disagreed and explained to her, "It doesn't matter if you're in a wheelchair; you'll always be the captain. You may not be able to perform the routines and the jumps, but we still need you to be a cheerleader, and have your pom-poms. You can cheer from your chair!"

Patricia appreciated these sweet words of affirmation from her peers, but, she still felt sad and a bit left out. But, she decided to go to practice after school.

After practice, Patricia's dad came to get her in the new customized van, along with the electric wheelchair, which had just been delivered. Christina and Patricia playfully enjoyed pushing the levers and turning the knobs on the new chair.

Patricia gleamed with excitement and shared with her father everything that had transpired during the day. Her father expressed his feelings toward his daughter as he turned to look at her. He told her just how very proud of her he was.

They continued an earlier conversation of how they were looking to find an assistant for Patricia, someone who could help her in the restroom, at her locker, and in the classroom.

Tuesday, Patricia became angry. She hurled her lunch tray and her books across the cafeteria. She was very angry because none of the students assisted her with her lunch tray. After the incident, Patricia was sent to the principal's office. Mrs. Jackson called Patricia's parents and asked them to come and get her.

This angered Patricia even more and she screamed and yelled at the principal. "I hate this *stupid* school! I hate *everyone* in this stupid school!"

Mrs. Jackson firmly suggested that Patricia calm down and relax. It was time to consider visiting with the school counselor down the hall. Patricia ignored the principal, still speaking loudly and angrily, tossing her arms around in frustration. She was quite vocal in her decision not to go see the school counselor.

"Patricia," said Mrs. Jackson, with authority in her voice. "I am still the principal of this school, young lady, and I am asking you to get yourself together and lower your voice."

Mrs. Jackson reached for her desk phone. She called Pastor Hanson in front of Patricia to see if he were available to come to the school immediately. Brian agreed and drove to the school. Upon entering the front office a few minutes later, he heard Patricia's loud and obnoxious words resonating in the walls.

Brian and the principal stooped down in front of Patricia in hopes of getting her to calm down. Patricia began to cry. She started to relax and Brian noticed that she seemed tired of screaming and yelling.

A few minutes later, Sue Anne and Clifford Miller arrived. When she saw her parents, Patricia began yelling again. "Why did you call my parents? I don't want them here!"

Clifford boldly stated, "You need to calm down, young lady. I want you to apologize to the adults in the room. We are only here to try to help you."

Sue Anne grabbed Patricia's hand to try to comfort her. Brian gently took Patricia's other hand. Patricia then slowly, through her tears, apologized to Mrs. Jackson and everyone for her behavior. She knew she'd messed up; yet, she was still an emotional mess inside. In that moment, Patricia knew she needed to make some changes — changes to her inner self.

Mrs. Jackson thanked Patricia for her apology and said she accepted it. She then stood up from behind her desk and politely explained to Patricia that she was suspended for the remainder of the day because of her inappropriate outbursts.

Sue Anne, Clifford, and Brian left Mrs. Jackson's office. Clifford reached for Brian's hand and thanked him for coming. They all headed outside. Brian reached over and placed his hand on Patricia's hand.

"We are here to help you, Patricia. Let us help you. It takes all of us, but, we love you and we want the best for you. Go see your counselor soon. Take care of yourself, young lady."

Patricia's parents scheduled an appointment with her counselor the following morning. Patricia explained to her counselor that overall she was happy to return to school, but she was still hoping to make more friends.

She shared with the counselor that only two friends had visited during her stay at the hospital. But, even bigger than the friendship issue was the fact that Patricia still had a lot of pain and anger. After all, she was still angry with Alan for wrecking the car and causing her injuries.

She explained to her counselor that she wanted to take the necessary steps toward healing and forgiveness. She was willing to remain in counseling as long as necessary.

The counselor took some notes and continued to listen to Patricia speak. After their one-hour session, she suggested scheduling several more weekly sessions.

The next morning, Brian shared his message to the students around the flagpole. As he glanced around the crowd of students, he nodded to acknowledge Patricia. Afterwards, she maneuvered her wheelchair around the other students. She gave Brian a hug.

"You're my best friend, Pastor Brian. I thank you for everything you and your family have done for me. I could not have gotten through these past months without your help and prayers," Patricia said sincerely.

Patricia paused for a brief moment and then told Brian that she was going to remain on the cheerleading team and that the others on the cheer team wanted her to continue to be the team captain. Brian smiled, telling her he was pleased with the news. Then, he noticed that someone was standing alongside the wheelchair, to aid Patricia.

"I'd like to introduce you to Gertrude, Pastor Brian. She is 25 and she is my aide. She's gonna help me get around because she's been trained to help people like me who have a disability," Patricia said, grinning as she made the introductions.

Overall, Patricia seemed to be adjusting well to being back at school. And, she was making adjustments in living her life and doing her daily routines from a wheelchair. Brian was concerned as to how she was emotionally handling her new status.

One day, Patricia was summoned to report to the front office. She was still behind with classwork and Mrs. Jackson explained to her that she would not be able to graduate with her class unless she could get caught up. The goal was for Patricia to attend summer school so she could earn enough credits to finish.

Patricia was slightly disappointed to know that she was behind; yet, she was a bit bummed to hear of the news regarding summer school.

She casually asked Mrs. Jackson if she would be able to graduate with her class on time if she worked hard. Principal Jackson was not sure and stated she'd check with the school registrar and the school counselor regarding all the requirements for graduation.

Patricia seemed a bit down after the conversation with the principal. Gertrude looked Patricia in the eye and calmly spoke to her as she touched Patricia's arm and reminded her that they were just taking one day at a time. Gertrude affirmed that she'd be there for Patricia every step of the way to see that Patricia would graduate on time with her class.

Monday morning, Gloria, Christina, and Alysia approached Pastor Brian after the morning devotion. They explained to him that Patricia was still having outbursts in class and that the teachers would ask her to leave the classroom.

The girls were concerned that Patricia was probably still feeling badly about her condition because she was still acting aloof and snobbish. They shared their genuine concern with their youth pastor, who listened intently as the teens revealed concern for their friend.

The following Monday, Patricia returned to school and went to the office. Mrs. Jackson informed her that she'd still not received all the details regarding what all Patricia would need to accomplish to graduate on time.

As Patricia was leaving the principal's office, she apologized for her behavior last week. She felt remorseful, yet, was still troubled on the inside, not sure why she was having emotional outbursts.

Christina approached Patricia after they left Mrs. Jackson's office. She asked with a kindness in her voice if everything was all right. Patricia shared with Christina that it was still a bit uncertain if Patricia would be graduating with her class. And, she told Christina that summer school was now on her calendar.

Christina nodded gently and smiled. She reminded Patricia that God was still in control and now was the time to truly trust Him. Christina laid her hand on Patricia's shoulder.

"You know, Patricia. We've been friends since kindergarten. You are still my friend and I love you. I'm here with you. I'm not goin' anywhere. We will get through this together," she reminded Patricia.

Johnny had joined them. He stood quietly through the friend-to-friend conversation. His politeness was evident as he allowed the teens to talk together. Patricia looked at Johnny and Christina and softly thanked each of them for being her friend.

Patricia then headed off to her first period class. Suddenly, an attractive new guy locked eyes with her. He introduced himself as Joseph Peterson.

Joseph had brown hair and eyes. He smiled at Patricia. "I'm the new quarterback this year. I just moved here a few months ago. What's your name?"

Patricia was a bit taken aback. A quick thought raced through her mind, "Who would be interested in me? I'm in a wheelchair."

Joseph continued smiling at Patricia. He continued, "I don't know many people. But, I'd like to go out this weekend. Maybe to a pizza place or something. Will you go with me?"

Patricia's face lit up. "Yes, I'd be glad to go with you."

"Okay, then. It's a date. Let's talk more later this week. I need to run to class," Joseph grinned, as he headed for class. Patricia was still a bit stunned. She had a date to look forward to. Suddenly, she felt wanted and liked.

Patricia glanced up and saw Johnny at his locker. "Hey, Johnny! You never told me how soccer and track are going."

Johnny responded with a grin on his face. "I'm on the first string in soccer, and I finally have some great friends on the team." He shared with Patricia that he was in the average range in track but that he still wanted to remain on the team and try to improve. And, he wished that his grades were better. He confided in Patricia that his current grade point average was a 2.5, and he was really hoping to improve academically this semester.

Johnny then shared with Patricia about his plans to attend college. He said he really wanted to get a major in psychology. He asked Patricia if she had plans to attend college.

"I'm not sure yet," Patricia stated, as she glanced up at Gertrude. Suddenly, Patricia realized that if she did go to college, she'd need help from Gertrude.

Patricia and Gertrude then headed to class. Suddenly, Patricia seemed annoyed. She began yelling at Gertrude and screaming, seemingly for no apparent reason. All the students wondered what had just occurred to make Patricia have such an emotional outburst.

Gertrude leaned down and began to talk to Patricia calmly and softly. Patricia settled down a bit, but, then, decided to throw her textbook across the room.

Gertrude was baffled, yet, handled the situation with grace and quickly escorted Patricia out of the room. By the time they got to the front office, Mrs. Jackson had already learned of the behavior and sent Patricia home for the day.

The next morning Patricia's parents were scheduled to see the doctor about her outbursts in school. They believed the counseling sessions were helpful overall, yet, they were still concerned about Patricia's behavior at school.

Clifford was concerned that there may be some deep emotional needs to address. And, Patricia had stayed home from school that morning, stating that she had no interest in school.

Her dad was perplexed as to her desire to remain home; however, he made a few quick calls and, that afternoon, her parents were able to get her in to see her doctor.

They believed that something could be wrong with Patricia, as they'd never seen her exhibit these types of behaviors before the accident. They were eager to see what the doctor said and to learn if some sort of evaluation or test were necessary to determine what was going on.

The doctor's evaluation was quite thorough. After he checked Patricia and asked her numerous questions, he asked to meet with her parents in the lobby.

He informed them that he believed Patricia suffered from a condition called intermittent explosive disorder or IED. He was concerned that she'd need medications to help regulate her mood swings. He said that this type of disorder is very common with people who have suffered intense trauma.

He reminded her parents also that Patricia qualified for a special type of therapy. He handed her parents a business card of a colleague whom he recommended.

The next morning at the flagpole, Brian delivered a message to the students about the value of lasting friendships. He shared from the New International Version of the Bible in Luke 11:8, "I tell you, even though he will not get up and give you the bread because of friendship, yet because of your shameless audacity he will surely get up and give you as much as you need."

Patricia and Johnny glanced at each other and smiled. Patricia had finally realized that Johnny was a true friend. After all, he'd been there with her through the ups and downs.

Brian encouraged the students to love and respect one another as equals in the eyes of God. He reminded them that Jesus commands them to love each other and that there's no room for hatred.

He said that friendship goes deep; it doesn't just depend on emotions or what's happening in someone's life at the moment. True friendship, he added, was a genuine, caring, and loving commitment toward someone, just as Jesus cares for each of us.

The students listened intently. Brian thanked God that the teens were tuned in to his words. And, Brian believed in his heart that there was about to be a breakthrough at the high school.

He believed God was doing something big in forging new and lasting friendships. And, maybe, just maybe, God had just started the movement with Patricia and Johnny?

CHAPTER 19: GRADUATION AND NEW BLESSINGS

*I*t was already May and almost time for graduation. Brian wasn't ready for Gloria to graduate this year. Where had the time gone? And, Brian couldn't believe that Patrick was following close behind on the heels of Gloria, due to graduate himself the following spring.

Gloria was excited about her college acceptance letter. She had wanted to be a teacher since she was a little girl, and she always enjoyed playing teacher with her younger sister, Stephanie. Now her dream would come true. She was eager to enjoy her summer and head off to college to begin preparing for her teaching career.

It was truly a bittersweet time for the Hanson household. Brian and Susan had just the night before shared with their teens that a new baby was on the way. Everyone cried tears of joy together, knowing that a new addition to the family would mean that God had not forgotten about their pain of losing Stephanie. Gloria was overjoyed to once again be a big sister and promised to come home from college often to see the new baby. Patrick, too, was thrilled, and he had difficulty gaining his composure after Brian shared with the teens. Patrick stated maturely that he knew God was still looking over them and that Stephanie, too, would have been so proud of her new status of big sister.

Brian was busy writing a graduation speech to share with the seniors. He'd grown to love this class. After all, these seniors had bonded through many struggles and he was quite proud of their maturity. He was proud of their willingness to stand for what was right. He was proud of their attendance at the flagpole each morning. And, mostly, he was proud of the teens for reaching out to Patricia and Johnny after the two had returned to school.

Monday, during Science class with Mrs. Rawlings, Mrs. Jackson pinged the teacher to please request that Patricia come to the office. Patricia and Gertrude looked at each other. They were concerned as to what the visit was about.

Patricia asked Gertrude with confusion in her eyes, "Did I do something wrong?" Gertrude quietly explained to Patricia that she didn't think so, but, maybe the conversation was about graduation. The two then left the class to head to the office.

Mrs. Jackson raised up from her desk to motion for the two to come into the office.

Patricia blurted out, "Did I do something wrong, Principal Jackson?"

Mrs. Jackson quietly closed the door and walked over to Patricia. She was smiling as she sat down next to Patricia.

"I am so very proud of you, Patricia. I have some good news for you," Mrs. Jackson said, smiling. "You have earned enough credits to graduate on time with your class. And, I wish to inform you of the best news of all — you have achieved the role of class valedictorian. Your overall grade point average is exceptional," the principal added, as she reached out to touch Patricia's hand.

Patricia's eyes grew wide as she placed her right hand over her mouth in amazement. Tears of joy rolled down her face. Gertrude, too, was teary eyed. Silence filled the room.

"Oh, my goodness, I can't believe this is happening."

"I am so very proud of you, Patricia. Your hard work and determination paid off. You are truly an overcomer. You are a role model. In spite of your physical struggles, you have studied hard and remained focused. I am so very pleased with all of your accomplishments," Mrs. Jackson said, beaming at both Patricia and Gertrude.

Patricia reached for Gertrude's hand and the two friends smiled together. In that moment, Patricia realized that she was indeed a strong person. She knew deep down inside that God had been with her over the past few months. She knew she had God to thank for this very moment; this moment where she was being recognized for staying on course, even when she hadn't felt like it. And, she realized too that being strong was truly more than feeling strong; it was a choice she'd made where her feelings hadn't lined up.

Suddenly, Patricia knew she needed to call Pastor Brian right away and share the good news with him. But, she knew she should tell her parents first.

After cheer practice that day, Patricia was eager to share with her parents the exciting news. Clifford pulled up in front of the school to pick up his daughter. She was waving her arms with excitement. Clifford stepped outside the van to help Gertrude with the wheelchair and noticed that Patricia had a big grin on her face. Clifford asked his daughter if there was something she wanted to share with him.

"Daddy! I have some awesome news to tell you and Mother when we get home! I hope I can wait that long! Let's go home!"

Patricia thanked Gertrude for helping her. Gertrude smiled and said she'd see Patricia first thing the next day.

When Patricia and her dad arrived home, Sue Anne was waiting in the living room. Clifford walked in behind his daughter, who had quickly maneuvered her wheelchair in front of her mother.

"Mom! Guess what? Mrs. Jackson told me today that I am going to be the class valedictorian! Can you believe it?" Patricia was still overjoyed with excitement.

Sue Anne was thrilled and quickly leaned over to her daughter to hug her tightly. She was thinking to herself that it was God who had made this happen for her daughter. She knew God had not left them in their time of need. She knew that God was a good Father, no matter anyone's circumstances.

Brian was thrilled with the news. Patricia was almost giddy as she spoke with him on her phone. It was still almost too good to be true for Patricia. Brian reminded her that all good things are from the Father above, who never forsakes His children.

At the flagpole the next day, while Brian spoke with Patricia and Gertrude, he noticed that Johnny was approaching him. Johnny and Christina had heard Patricia's exciting news and decided to share their news with Brian.

Johnny said he wanted to attend college after graduation. He was going to miss his friends who were graduating this year. He said he'd miss Christina while she was away at college for her freshman year. But, he wanted to continue to date her and hoped to marry her one day. Johnny was thrilled about Christina's plans to study sociology and become a high school teacher.

Saturday morning, Susan had an appointment with her obstetrics doctor. She and Brian had decided that they were okay with learning the gender of the baby before it was born. They were eager to know if their precious gift from God would be a boy or a girl. They had not requested an early gender reveal with the other children; they'd just waited until the moment each was born. But, this time things were different. Their lives were different. And, all the Hansons had a longing to see what God would be adding to their family. They knew God had a blessing in store for them.

Susan and Brian were a bit nervous when they walked into the doctor's office. The nurse performed a sonogram as Brian held Susan's hand. The doctor came in just as the nurse completed the test. He looked at the computer screen and smiled.

"Your baby is a girl," the doctor said calmly, with a grin on his face. "She looks to be healthy and growing right on target."

Susan was extremely emotional and started sobbing. Brian sensed a bittersweet atmosphere. He knew that the remainder of this pregnancy would evoke sad thoughts of Stephanie as well as bring great joy to his wife and kids.

Susan and Brian held hands in silence for a few moments. They spoke softly and agreed to go out for lunch to spend time together. And, Susan stated happily that she was ready to begin thinking of names for her new baby girl.

After school, Brian asked his teens to convene in the living room. He and Susan shared that the baby was a girl. The teens were ecstatic. Susan mentioned that she wanted all of them to start considering names. Gloria was soon to head out of town on her senior trip to South Dakota. Her dad reminded her to be careful, and, added, a bit teasingly for her to be sure to take time to think of some names she'd like for her baby sister.

Brian put his arm around Susan. He was peaceful and content. He knew God was planning great things for his family during this time of great transition.

Several days later, after Gloria and the senior class had returned from a great time away, the Hansons once again met in the living room to discuss the baby. Patrick was the first to break the ice.

"Well, we could name the baby 'It'," he said jokingly. They all laughed in unison.

"No, Patrick," said Susan. "We are not naming the baby 'It'."

Patrick couldn't stop laughing until Susan yelled, "Please be serious and come up with a name." Patrick agreed and apologized to his mother.

"What about Carrie or Glenda?" Patrick again started laughing and before he was able to get a word out, Gloria picked up a pillow and started hitting him.

Gloria tried to bring the conversation back around to a serious note.

"What about Deborah or maybe Chrystal?" She also liked the names her brother picked out.

Brian knew it was time for him to throw in his two cents worth. He said he liked the names Amanda and Samantha. Susan pondered a moment, thinking of the names Brian mentioned.

"I like these names: Katie, Renea, and Ruth," Susan had an idea to stop the seemingly endless discussion of names. She stood up and headed to the kitchen. Her family had no idea what she was up to.

In the kitchen, Susan wrote all the possible names on small pieces of paper and then placed them in a bowl. She then stirred the names several times and continued stirring the papers with her hand as she walked back into the living room.

Her family looked at her as she stirred and stirred.

"It's time, you guys," Susan stated dramatically as she took her hand out of the bowl. "Let's choose a name for our new little one." With their eyes stationed intently on the bowl, they waited for Susan to choose a paper, unfold it, and announce the name.

"Well, here it is. Your new baby sister will be called Deborah," Susan said as she sighed heavily and with a grin on her face. "I'm glad that's over!"

Brian was thrilled. He knew that Deborah, mentioned in the Old Testament, was a woman of God — a woman whose very name meant "bee." Deborah was both a heroine and a prophetess, in charge of an army that was victorious in battle.

The following Monday, Gloria landed a part-time job, waiting tables at a local diner. She wanted to take the summer off and hang out with her friends, but she also really wanted to earn some spending money for college. She knew that having a job would be good experience. Her parents were proud of her eagerness to work and her intrinsic determination and drive.

It was now just a week away from graduation. The seniors were eagerly awaiting the end of school. They were ready to start their summer jobs and prepare for college or begin their careers.

An excitement filled the air — a great anticipation of what was yet to come — at the high school, around the flagpole each day, and at youth group on Wednesday nights. It was refreshing for Brian to witness what all was happening in these young people's lives. After all, they had the rest of their lives ahead of them.

Brian had a brief, informal conversation with Mrs. Jackson in the hall after the morning devotional at the flagpole. He was eager to tell her that Susan was expecting a baby. The principal was thrilled with the news and she had some news of her own. She said that she was retiring from her role as principal. Brian hinted, with a smile on his face, that he believed Susan would make a good principal someday, possibly after their new child began attending school.

He shook the principal's hand and congratulated her on her upcoming retirement. He replied that he'd get back to her after he and Susan talked about the possible new role as assistant principal. He knew Susan would need to make a big commitment to such a demanding role — a role that she may turn down since she would soon be a mom of a newborn.

Principal Jackson smiled, thanking Pastor Hanson for being instrumental to all the students. Then she said how she was quite grateful for his role as an encourager and how he had inspired the students. She thanked him too for his unwavering spirit and for being a source of godly strength for the teens, not only in the high school, but in the entire community.

The enrollment records were released from administration, revealing that 749 seniors would graduate. The time came to prepare for the big event. Student council members set up chairs in precise rows in the gym. The stage was decorated for staff and select teachers who were presenting diplomas and awards.

Out of honor and in memory of their classmate, Alan, who had died in the car accident, the student council posed a picture and a wreath in the first seat on the center aisle on the front row. Here everyone seated in the gym could see the memorial, which was designed to pay tribute to their great friend.

Patricia was prepared to address the crowd with her valedictorian speech. She knew it would be the largest crowd she'd ever stood in front of; but, she'd already prayed and asked God to speak through her and to use her to speak to others. She was prepared; yet, nervous at the same time.

Brian reminded Susan to record a video on her cell phone. He did not want to miss getting his daughter's accomplishment recorded. The massive sea of teens lined up to march in was quite overwhelming to Brian. The graduation regalia consisted of gowns, caps, and tassels in Wildcat blue and gold.

The crowd of bold colors resembled a huge field of spring wildflowers. After all, it was truly springtime in the lives of these young people. They were now emerging as new baby butterflies, ready to fly out into the world and ready to go forth and do great things. Brian quietly prayed over the crowd, asking God to give each and every teen His wisdom and discernment for their new lives away from the comfort and routine of high school.

It was time for Patricia to give her speech. She maneuvered herself up to the podium where the staff person before her had just completed the invocation and lowered the mic. Patricia leaned in and spoke. The vast room filled with immediate silence.

> *"In this moment, as we take a moment to be proud of ourselves, our friends, our parents, and loved ones, I bring to you a message of humility. In a time of disintegration, diminished values, fragmented principles, and lack of focus, I dare to call your attention to this precious moment. It was only twelve short years ago when you crossed the threshold and walked into your first school. That first day of school was, for some, an ominous cloud; for others, was an opportunity to chase a rainbow.*
>
> *"You knew, however, that there were people to cheer you on and help you get through both your school day and all the school years that would follow. Some of you remember the early morning "good-byes" from your parents and how you felt loved when, once again, you'd see your parent or parents waiting for you at the end of the school day.*

'Then, the homework began to become a normal part of life. Some of us perceived homework to be a chore; others believed it to be an opportunity to learn.

"Four years have passed since you felt that the peak of achievement waited for you in the high school classrooms. And here you are today, wondering what is next. There is pride in your eyes, hope in your hearts, and plans for your future in your minds. Pride, hope, and future plans are well deserved and achievable.

"Let's savor this moment today as a marker in our lives. A marker of a huge accomplishment. An item to check off of our bucket lists, such as skydiving over a majestic canyon or hiking in the Alps. Let's remember that to achieve those things we dream of, we must remain humble, focused and determined, and not choose to be the one always in the limelight. Even though we have goals and dreams, we must learn that good leaders are servant leaders; they lead by example.

"The thrill of a skydive or a hike in the mountains certainly is a high to remember. But, these accomplishments that we achieve musts come as we pursue humility. Neither pride nor boastfulness is a strategy for winning others over; rather, humility in itself is a huge characteristic of a great leader.

"To pursue humility is to understand that the world is not always looking at you. The world really couldn't care less about our accomplishments. But, remember, the world is impressed when we reach outstanding peaks with humility — a humility that outshines our sweat and tears.

"In a world of interminable wars, terroristic activities, famine, and need, you here today have been privileged to be exposed to the greatest of all: diverse cultures, friendships across vast territories, of famine amidst incomparable wealth, you have been privileged to be exposed to the greatest of all diversities: That of cultures, habits, languages, attitudes and patterns of behavior.

"As we all know, very few schools in the world can boast of the enormous diversity of nationalities found here at Millsville High School. We are the Wildcats and we are strong. We are a generation

of multinational, and, dare I say, transnational individuals, whose ability to cope with and celebrate diversity is second to none. Tolerance and understanding are the most effective antidotes to prejudice. Like a parachute, your mind functions better because it is open. And, as the properties and technology of an electronic device, you carry in your heads a myriad of sounds and images that will shape the choices you will make in the near future. The way that you've seen diversity here in this place has already given you a foundation for boldly facing our great world.

"However, nothing will replace your personal and intrinsic principles, values, and ethical and moral decisions. Through your decisions, our decisions, we will build the future of our world. We are the generation to go forth and shine like no other generation before us.

"And, as we go and conquer, we must remember that nothing will take away the relationships that we find to be dear: our families, our friends, and our classmates. And, nothing will be greater in our lives than being fair and just, understanding and courageous, and bold — all in the face of adversity.

"Courage, my friends, is not the absence of fear. Only idiots have no fear. Courage is the mastering of fear. Master your fear, be humble, aim higher, live your dreams, be fair and just, remembering not solely where you are going, but, particularly, where you came from. One day, you will look at the education you received and the experiences you built in this great school. You will realize that here you gained a great foundation on which to build your future.

"Here, we have all built our characters within the framework of integrity. Yes, the best is yet to come. Yes, we will face trials and struggles. Yes, the world may be cruel around us. But, we all have this one thing in common: the knowledge that we together, as a class, will right now savor the moment! Congratulations, seniors!"

Patricia presented her words eloquently and smoothly, as if she'd prepared for this day for many years. She was very polished and mature. Brian glanced to the left to study the faces of Patricia's parents. He knew they were so very pleased of their daughter's accomplishments in spite of the physical and emotional pain and anguish she'd suffered. Brian smiled to himself, vowing to continue to pray for Patricia and her parents.

Patricia ended her speech just as an accomplished politician would have, with the crowd applauding and cheering.

Tina, as salutatorian, was next to present her speech. She walked up to the podium after the applause faded. She paused a moment to raise the mic up to her face, as her words began to flow over the crowd.

After she shared her speech, Tina paused a moment to enjoy the great applause. She smiled as she scanned the audience. Then, she returned to her seat on the stage, next to Patricia.

Then came the moment where Mrs. Jackson and other school officials began passing out diplomas as each graduate approached center stage. After all the graduates were back in their rows and seated, Principal Jackson asked them to all stand.

They all stood to move their tassels over to the other side of their caps. On cue, the band played the closing song of celebration. The students exited their rows in pairs to leave the seating area. Then, like a massive uproar, the graduates tossed their caps high into the air. It seemed as if a huge bag of caps and tassels had just been set off by fireworks. The room was filled with color, cheer, and excitement.

Afterwards, as they celebrated, making photos and videos, they began forming groups with their families and friends, Brian spoke to Susan, sharing that Mrs. Jackson had announced her retirement.

Brian met up with his daughter and her friends. He gave Gloria a big hug. "I'm proud of you, Gloria. I am proud too to be your dad. You have no idea how very proud of you I am. Your mother, too, is proud of you. We just know you will do great things in your life."

Several students came over to give Pastor Hanson a hug and thank him. Patricia wheeled over with some of the students and she was holding a small gift box. She looked at Brian and smiled.

"Pastor, we have a little something for you," she said, revealing the box.

Brian was a bit stunned for a moment. He reached out to take the box from Patricia and thanked the students for thinking of him in such a kind way.

To his surprise, there inside the purple velvet lining was a silver pocket watch. He lifted it carefully out of the box and read its inscription aloud to the students around him. It was engraved *"A Friend I Didn't Know."*

Johnny was the first to speak up. He was a bit puzzled.

"Pastor Brian, what does the watch mean? I'm not sure I'm getting it," Johnny confessed.

Brain looked at the students around him. He waited patiently for someone to respond. Patricia explained to Johnny as the others listened intently that the watch represented all the friendships that had formed in the past year. She added that the watch also represented the admiration the students had for Pastor Brian and his leadership.

Johnny still wore a look of confusion on his face regarding the choice of words inscribed on the watch.

Brian wanted to leave the students with a lasting heartfelt message. He wanted to leave an impression on their hearts; a lasting impression that they'd never forget; one that would forever remind them of this special time. The students began looking at each other with a puzzled glaze.

Brian turned toward Patricia and began sharing a few of his observations from the past year.

"Patricia, you believed that you could gain more friends by being popular, right?" he asked her. Patricia nodded affirmatively and grinned. "Yes," she replied. "And, I thought being on the cheer team was the way to get popular."

Then, Brian turned and addressed Johnny. "You thought you could make more friends at school through your achievements and sports, correct?" Johnny smiled in agreement. "Yeah, but, now I know that those things don't really matter that much, Pastor."

Brian went on, knowing this was his final message of the school year to the students about the value of friendships and the bonds that friends share.

As Brian began to speak to the teens gathered around him, more students showed up to listen in. Brian pondered a moment to gather his thoughts, waiting on the Holy Spirit to give him the right words to share. He glanced down a moment to focus his attention on the lovely pocket watch the students had given him.

"We all seem to place value and sentimentality on material objects such as this watch," he said, looking across the crowd. "However, over the years, the tarnish tends to wear off. This object one day will no longer be as shiny as it is now. It will no longer look new and impressive.

"And, similarly, the friendships we share with each other may not remain as close as they are today," Brian continued, eloquently.

"You guys here today — Johnny, Patricia, you others — we will always have our memories of our friends whom we leave behind. And, we will make new friends as time goes on.

"But, young people, listen up," Brian continued, glancing over the crowd. The students were intently looking back at him.

"That one true friend who we will always have with us will never leave us," Brian emphasized. "Our one true friend, the One whom God sent to us many, many years ago, was His Son. God's plan was for us to get to know His Son, Jesus. Jesus is the friend we didn't know we ever had. The Bible says that Jesus will stick closer to us than a brother."

Brian took the watch out of the box. He clipped the chain carefully to his belt loop and slipped the watch into his pocket. He then looked up at the teens, smiling.

His countenance was calm, yet radiant. He was so very proud of the group of young people assembled around him. He just knew God would use each and every one of them in a big way.

"You know, guys, it's all about Jesus. He wants to be the one true friend whom you didn't know you ever had."

There's Hope for You Today!

Whoever you are and wherever you are, God has not left you alone. There is hope for you! Our God loves you very much. He even knew you'd be reading this book about hope!

We all have struggled to find hope and peace from bullying, negative thoughts, discouragement and other things.

There is no simple solution in today's world to stop all the ugliness, but, we have a God who loves us all. He loves you. He loves me. We must allow God, the Author of Love, to work through us to help us press on and overcome. We must work together in harmony and peace.

Our goal must be to encourage each other. We must show kindness. You never know who may need a word of encouragement or a gesture of kindness from you.

We must work, united, to find solutions for today's problems. Let's build relationships based on listening, learning, and caring. Let's use our voices and abilities to fight bullying and suicide and other things that affect our youth today. Let's be willing to speak up in difficult situations.

When you feel that there is no one there for you, there *IS* always someone who cares about you. Someone is always thinking about you and praying for you.

Please, connect with others. Let God lead you to people who can help you. After all, our God is a God of Hope!

"For I know the plans I have for you,"
declares the LORD,
"Plans to prosper you and not to harm you,
plans to give you hope and a future."
Jeremiah 29:11 NIV

TESTIMONIALS

The following testimonials are from real people — people just like you and me who have experienced bullying, depression, and suicidal thoughts.

The actual names have been removed to protect their true identities.

"In the fifth grade, I was bullied because of my weight. I was called many names such as "fat," "blob," and "meatball." All of those words were very mean and they always hurt me.

Most of the time, I'd start a verbal and physical fight with the accusers. Sometimes this would result in school suspension and detention. Bullying is not something to be proud of and someone will always be harmed by it."

Male, age 14, Texas, USA

"My daughter and I wore purple for her today. It was her favorite color, but there was so much more. Her visitation was packed. So many friends and family. Surely she knew she was loved. Surely she knew. I wonder if that was enough. I wonder why. We all wonder why. Twenty-two years old. So much of life ahead of her.

I am over twice her age now and I have seen what life brings. There are so many moments of amazing joy. There is sorrow, too, of course. But the wonder of life prevails. I wish I could relate that to someone who believes they are on the edge. I wish I could fix it. It's all complicated and filled with mystery. In the end, however, there is only absence."

Male, age 54, Missouri, USA

"My son is in 7th grade. Just three 3 days into the school year, he was already being bullied. He gets picked on, called names, hit, and spit on. He's even dreamed about the way other students treat him.

"There's nothing I can do about it. I've been immobile for two years because of my health. I just feel so badly for my son."

Female, age 40, Missouri, USA

"I had a pretty normal childhood. I was raised in a Christian family and we attended church regularly. When I went to high school, life turned into a downward spiral. After numerous suicide attempts, I was finally HEALED of clinical depression. I wanted to secure my future on earth and in heaven. This meant I'd have to do well in school so I could obtain a great job. And, I wasn't sure what would define me as a Christian. I thought as long as you're forgiven of sin and are involved in church and ministry, you won't go to hell.

I had to make sure I'd never sin; or, at least that I'd be forgiven of sin, but how would I do that? I decided to pay close attention to the testimonies of older kids in my church, and I noticed a pattern. It seemed that everyone who wanted to fit in began drinking and smoking. If I wanted to remain 'saved' that I probably shouldn't try to fit in. So, that's what I did. But, once I began high school, and the other students noticed that I wasn't trying to fit in, they began to bully me. The entire school knew me, and everyone thought I was weird and different. It didn't help that I was small for my age. I began to feel different, so different, that I no longer believed I was human. I began to doubt that my parents were really my parents and I began to make up conspiracy theories as to why my life was a lie.

In my sophomore year, the bullying became worse and turned physical. One day a bully held me up at knifepoint. I went home and told my mom. The next day at school, the bully asked if I had told anyone. I was scared that if I told him the truth, he might kill me. I told him I hadn't. One of my classmates, a Muslim, was standing behind the bully. He said, "He's telling the truth. He's a Christian."

The following weeks I received online death threats and I was transferred to a Christian school. I got bullied again. Fights were common for me, and I usually didn't fight back because I feared I wouldn't stop and would accidentally kill someone.

My junior year, my father's health rapidly declined and he was hospitalized. The doctors put him on a treatment to fight his hepatitis. The list of side effects is long, and suicide and murder are possible side effects. I witnessed my father change because of the medication. I soon no longer felt safe at home; the one place I had always been safe. Between my home life and the school bullying, I felt as if I didn't belong anywhere. I didn't do well at school. I developed social anxiety. I was too scared to raise my hand in class, talk to more than five people, or speak to girls.

I also developed a form of dissociation, which led to partial amnesia as well as severe depression. I got so depressed that I tried to drown myself, but I couldn't stay under water long enough. I turned to gaming, music, and writing as a way to escape the real world without disturbing anyone. I began to feel an immense hatred and bitterness toward my bullies. Eventually, I hated everyone except those I knew. I developed a lust for blood and wanted to kill anyone who'd ever done me wrong. In college I was bullied again. I got into the school's first-ever fight. One day, I rode my bike home from work. I felt depressed and wasn't in a hurry to get home. Everything in my life became too much for me to handle.

A train track was to the right of me, and in a split second I decided to ride in front of an oncoming train. What I didn't realize was that there was a sidetrack at this particular spot. So, the train drove right past me. Had God interfered? I began to think about God's plan again and the purpose of life. I wondered: was this a coincidence? Had God interfered? I'd known of God's existence, but depression had devoured me. I didn't care if I died.

I chose to let Jesus into my life, and to no longer try to fight the war on my own. After I prayed the sinner's prayer, I joined the church drama team and youth choir. I was the shy kid with social anxiety; yet soon I landed a solo to sing in front of 1,300 people. I still didn't know what it meant to really BE a Christian. When problems arose in my life, I'd pray if God would help me through. When He did, I said, 'Thanks God, I can take it from here.' I tried to live a good life, but eventually ended up as a hypocrite, living a double life.

I have never smoked, done drugs, nor drunk alcohol. But I didn't need to do these things to commit EVERY SIN that God mentions in His Word. Everything I once looked down on, I became. My life turned into the biggest nightmare. I had already tried to end my life. I'm not very good at suicide, so I decided not to try again.

Through everything I've been through, those persons whom I looked up to failed me. Those who were my friends betrayed me. So I began seeking God. I no longer wanted to rely on my works to secure my salvation. I wanted a relationship with the living God.

In my entire life, there was a constant whisper in my head telling me to never fully surrender to God. I feared God because I couldn't understand Him. But, I knew God was the only one who could give me true fulfillment. I finally surrendered. My prayer was, 'God, I surrender to You. I lay my life in Your hands, and I recognize Jesus as my Savior.' That was when God saved me. Trying to live a good life without surrendering to God never gave me the peace and joy I experience today. God also led me to forgive, which was one of the toughest struggles I've had after I got saved. But I'm glad to testify I have forgiven every person who has ever done me wrong."

Male, age 25, The Netherlands

ABOUT THE AUTHOR

Harel R. Lawrence, a Missouri native, is a Christian fiction author and substitute teacher. His goal is to create positive change in young people's lives through the power of creative storytelling. His work has been showcased in *Eyes on Magazine*, published in 2017. He has received numerous awards, including two in 2004, *Who's Who in Poetry* and *Editor's Choice Award.*

Harel authored the following books, available on Amazon: *Surviving the Night* (2017), *Riding on the Hearts of Love* (2016), and *Take a Closer Look: A Spiritual Journey into the Soul* (2002).

He has also released a music album, available on YouTube, iTunes, Amazon, and Spotify.

Harel holds an Associate of Science degree in law enforcement and a Bachelor of Science degree in criminal justice administration.

He is actively involved in his church, enjoys working with youth, and participates in short-term ministry trips in the United States and abroad.

Other Books by This Author

Surviving the Night

Riding on the Hearts of Love

Skye's High Fly'n Adventures: How Skye Gets His Name?

Take a Closer Look: A Spiritual Journey into the Soul

Made in the USA
Monee, IL
09 February 2021

59680567R00108